"DATA," THE BORG SAID TO HIM, "DO YOU HAVE A FRIEND?"

Data stopped and stared at the Borg. A friend. Inefficient phraseology, but he understood the vernacular.

"Yes," he said. "His name is Geordi."

The Borg's optical appliance shimmered. "Imagine Geordi standing in this room. If it meant you could feel emotions again, the way you did on Ohniaka Three, would you kill your friend? Would you kill Geordi?"

Data felt the hunger that burned in the heat of the sensations flooding him. He stared at the Borg and let himself be possessed by the orgiastic truth. He had always known he was strong, but now he knew he was dangerous, too. He had killed. And he had liked it.

"Yes," Data said calmly. "Yes, I would."

Look for STAR TREK Fiction from Pocket Books

Star Trek: The Original Series

Shadows on the Sun
Probe
Prime Directive
The Lost Years
Star Trek VI:
    The Undiscovered Country
Star Trek V:
    The Final Frontier
Star Trek IV:
    The Voyage Home
Spock's World
Enterprise
Strangers from the Sky
Final Frontier
#1 Star Trek:
    The Motion Picture
#2 The Entropy Effect
#3 The Klingon Gambit
#4 The Covenant of the Crown
#5 The Prometheus Design
#6 The Abode of Life
#7 Star Trek II:
    The Wrath of Khan
#8 Black Fire
#9 Triangle
#10 Web of the Romulans
#11 Yesterday's Son
#12 Mutiny on the Enterprise
#13 The Wounded Sky
#14 The Trellisane Confrontation
#15 Corona
#16 The Final Reflection
#17 Star Trek III:
    The Search for Spock
#18 My Enemy, My Ally
#19 The Tears of the Singers
#20 The Vulcan Academy Murders
#21 Uhura's Song
#22 Shadow Lord
#23 Ishmael
#24 Killing Time
#25 Dwellers in the Crucible

#26 Pawns and Symbols
#27 Mindshadow
#28 Crisis on Centaurus
#29 Dreadnought!
#30 Demons
#31 Battlestations!
#32 Chain of Attack
#33 Deep Domain
#34 Dreams of the Raven
#35 The Romulan Way
#36 How Much for Just the Planet?
#37 Bloodthirst
#38 The IDIC Epidemic
#39 Time for Yesterday
#40 Timetrap
#41 The Three-Minute Universe
#42 Memory Prime
#43 The Final Nexus
#44 Vulcan's Glory
#45 Double, Double
#46 The Cry of the Onlies
#47 The Kobayashi Maru
#48 Rules of Engagement
#49 The Pandora Principle
#50 Doctor's Orders
#51 Enemy Unseen
#52 Home Is the Hunter
#53 Ghost Walker
#54 A Flag Full of Stars
#55 Renegade
#56 Legacy
#57 The Rift
#58 Faces of Fire
#59 The Disinherited
#60 Ice Trap
#61 Sanctuary
#62 Death Count
#63 Shell Game
#64 The Starship Trap
#65 Windows on a Lost World
#66 From the Depths
#67 The Great Starship Race

Star Trek: The Next Generation

Descent
The Devil's Heart
Imzadi
Relics
Reunion
Unification
Metamorphosis
Vendetta
Encounter at Farpoint
#1 Ghost Ship
#2 The Peacekeepers
#3 The Children of Hamlin
#4 Survivors
#5 Strike Zone
#6 Power Hungry
#7 Masks
#8 The Captains' Honor
#9 A Call to Darkness

#10 A Rock and a Hard Place
#11 Gulliver's Fugitives
#12 Doomsday World
#13 The Eyes of the Beholders
#14 Exiles
#15 Fortune's Light
#16 Contamination
#17 Boogeymen
#18 Q-in-Law
#19 Perchance to Dream
#20 Spartacus
#21 Chains of Command
#22 Imbalance
#23 War Drums
#24 Nightshade
#25 Grounded
#26 The Romulan Prize
#27 Guises of the Mind

Star Trek: Deep Space Nine

#1 Emissary
#2 The Siege
#3 Bloodletter

STAR TREK®
THE NEXT GENERATION™

DESCENT

A NOVEL BY DIANE CAREY
BASED ON DESCENT, PART ONE
STORY BY JERI TAYLOR
TELEPLAY BY RONALD D. MOORE
AND
BASED ON DESCENT, PART TWO
WRITTEN BY RENÉ ECHEVARRIA

POCKET BOOKS
New York   London   Toronto   Sydney   Tokyo   Singapore

An *Original* Publication of POCKET BOOKS

POCKET BOOKS, a division of Simon & Schuster Inc. 1230 Avenue of the Americas, New York, NY 10020

Copyright © 1993 by Paramount Pictures. All Rights Reserved.

STAR TREK is a Registered Trademark of Paramount Pictures.

This book is published by Pocket Books, a division of Simon & Schuster Inc., under exclusive license from Paramount Pictures.

ISBN: 0-671-88267-8

First Pocket Books printing October 1993

10 9 8 7 6 5 4 3 2 1

POCKET and colophon are registered trademarks of Simon & Schuster Inc.

Printed in the U.S.A.

DESCENT

Chapter One

"... BUT THEN I SAID, 'In that frame of reference, the perihelion of Mercury would have precessed in the opposite direction.'"

The face that belonged to the buzzing voice was decorated with a wide smile and a flash of defiant life in a shriveled body huddled within the confines of a supportive chair.

Of the four men present, one had told the story and another now erupted in laughter.

A third frowned and pondered the anecdote, and the fourth ... was not a man.

"Dat is a great story!" The second fellow laughed, a haggard presence with a flying cloud of chalky hair, a mustache like a hanging horsehair brush, and a chopping German accent.

To the casual observer, the man who was not a man may have been amused—it was difficult to tell. Despite a face painted gold, as the face of a jester would be, there was painful poor entertainment in the bullion cheeks and the yellow eyes. He wore a hat brim with no hat, not even a plume, as if to shield those yellow eyes from the single source of light above their heads, and he was dealing very slick gaming cards to the gathering.

"Quite amusing, Dr. Hawking," the bullion one said. Now he shifted slightly and looked to his right. "You see, Sir Isaac, the joke depends on an understanding of the relativistic curvature of space-time. If two non-inertial reference frames are in relative motion—"

Puffing up his nobleman's pride, Professor of Mathematics and Knight of the Realm Sir Isaac Newton challenged the off-putting birdlike eyes of their dealer.

"Do not patronize me, sir," he said. "I invented physics. The day the apple fell on my head was the most momentous day in the history of science."

He resisted the urge to tell them that he had been on the edge of comprehending the story when they denied him the chance to think by their overexplaining. He would never do such to his students.

Across from him, the little debilitated scientist

struggled physically in his mobile chair and buzzed, "Not the apple story again."

Sir Isaac's lips fell open. He stared, and his mind hammered. He couldn't speak.

"That story is generally believed to be apocryphal," the metal-leaf one said bluntly, without the slightest courtesy.

Sir Isaac felt his chest constrict. "How dare you!"

The old man with the flying hair tapped his hand of slippery cards. "Perhaps we should return to the game." He shifted on an elbow and looked at Hawking. "Let's see. . . . You raised Mr. Data four, which means the bet is seven to me."

"The bet is ten!" Sir Isaac roared. "Can't you do simple arithmetic?"

Genius. Where?

They were playing with the cards and chips piled before them upon a round table covered with soft green fabric. There wasn't a single candle sconce on any wall to provide a sense of balance in the room. Only that light from above, which Sir Isaac reasoned must be mirrored sunlight.

How can they chortle at the past? Shall I chortle at the findings of Copernicus, Galileo, Kepler—even though I corrected their conclusions? Can any true scientist guffaw at the work of those who struggled before?

At once he paused, caught on this vague sense of future. Somehow he understood that these men around him were from *his* future, yet the understanding failed to shock him. These men talked about the future and the past arbitrarily, as though one did not stand invariably upon the bulwark of the other. Stephen Hawking could never be sitting in such a sophisticated contraption, with a mechanism holding his cards for him, had others not leaned on canes or been pulled in carts before him, compelled to find better ways.

Time again, future and present . . . How could these seem so liquid?

Feeling out of place, Sir Isaac regarded the others and fingered a ringlet of his chest-length tumble of curls. The others wore no wigs to hide their heads. And he was the only man here wearing appropriate scholars'-meeting attire. The others had no breeches or overcoats, no cravats, and there wasn't a sword or cane in sight. Perhaps these were their bedclothes.

Cloud-haired Einstein pushed a count of chips out to the center of the table.

Impatiently Sir Isaac matched the bet. "I don't know why I'm here in the first place," he muttered.

He had never been taught this game, but somehow he knew how to play it and was impelled to do so against his will. Certainly there were better things to do, more suitable subjects for four intelligent men to discuss than chips and folds, calls and bluffs. After all, he was warden of the mint. A professor at Cambridge University. A member of Parliament. A knight. And still these men had asked nothing about the binomial theorem or the method of fluxions as the basis of calculus, and they had laughed at his codification of the quantitative laws of universal dynamics.

They had laughed.

Was the future so smug? How could those who made use of a science chortle at those who revealed the science to mankind?

Wallowing in insult, he longed to get up and investigate the optics of that light abovehead to see if it conformed to his theories of spectral colors combining to form white light.

But he couldn't get up. Somehow he was forced from within to continue sitting, playing. Was this a dream?

As he held his cards in cold hands and dealt with the core of his fear that the church was wrong and this might be some sad afterlife, he cleared his throat. "What is the point of playing this ridiculous game?"

Mr. Data matched the bet and said, "Call. When I play poker with my shipmates, I often find that it is a useful forum for exploring different facets of humanity. I was curious to see how three of history's greatest minds would interact in this setting. So far it has proven most illuminating."

The old man looked at his own stack of chips. "And profitable."

Sir Isaac observed the others cannily but found little true brilliance evident here, with the exception of Stephen Hawking. The being called Data tended to explain details too much, and Einstein was obviously German.

Of course, this game they played was disinclined to show brilliance. Had Mr. Data wished to investigate brilliance, why not visit the grounds of Cambridge in 1707?

Apocryphal . . . Are my publications also apocryphal? How quick the future is to minimize the past. I am disappointed.

He felt distant vibration in the floor and wished to get up, to seek through the surrounding darkness and find the walls. Perhaps if he found a wall, he could discover what was behind it.

Yet he felt compelled to remain here and play this time-wasting game. What force had hold of him? He felt his curiosity begin to stultify. Would God Almighty wish him to sit and grow more stupid by the moment?

"Can we get this over with, please?" he urged. To Hawking he said, "It is your bet."

"I raise fifty," Hawking buzzed.

Mr. Data accommodated the debilitated participant by shoving out chips for him.

Sir Isaac threw his cards to the platform. "Blast! I fold."

The others seemed glad of it.

And he, too, was glad. Now he could sit here and deepen his thinking, rather than be some kind of reliquiae for their entertainment. He was a professor, not a farceur.

"The uncertainty principle will not help you now, Stephen," Einstein said in that halting accent. "All the quantum fluctuations in the universe won't change the cards in your hands. You are bluffing and you will lose."

"Wrong again, Albert," Hawking retorted. The robotic extension that was holding his cards for him slapped them face up on the table.

Four sevens.

Einstein scowled, then sat there and shook as he chuckled inwardly.

Sir Isaac watched as they played, particularly fascinated by Hawking and the mechanisms to which he was attached.

A man with Stephen's affliction in the 1600s, he thought, *would have no time for genius. And that is my commonality with him. He was stricken with this debilitation, and its only gift, for all it stole from him, was to give him time to think, to fill the emptiness with light. Time to move from brightness of mind to brilliance. I know the ache to fill such emptiness. When Cambridge was closed during the plague, those many months of sequestered thought allowed me to compose my most momentous theories. . . . Now we sit together, I from my time and Hawking from another. What would we all be if born in each other's time?*

And the old man named Einstein, had he lived in the 1600s, with that shabby demeanor and common clumsiness, would have been unable to find sustenance among the peasant class to which he was obviously born.

Sir Isaac had no doubt where this Mr. Data would be. Hanging from a spit, most like, being put to the torch by a shocked mob who thought he was a piece of bewitched cloisonné.

And who would I be in their time?

The floor began to vibrate. Sir Isaac looked around. He was sure he felt it—that it was not in his mind, and that he was in no dream. Suddenly the voice of heaven boomed around them, and he felt his hands grow even colder at its sound.

"Red Alert. All personnel report to duty stations. Red Alert. Repeat: Red Alert."

The others paused, but Mr. Data was the only one who did not appear confused. He stood, deposited his cards before him, and said, "We will have to continue this at another time."

Sir Isaac shifted his legs beneath him in preparation to stand. Where would he be expected to wait in this candleless world of vibrating voices and constant questions?

Hope pierced his unease. As long as there were questions, he would be no antiquary. Any scientist had purpose where there was any question.

"End program," Mr. Data said.

Sir Isaac tightened his thighs to stand, his gaze fixed upon the inhuman face of their dealer.

But he felt his own memory begin to dissolve. A touch of panic invaded his mind but found nothing to grasp.

The gold-leaf face grew dark before his eyes. For an instant there were amber lines in the form of a broad grid against the blackness.

Then . . . only blackness.

Chapter Two

U.S.S. Enterprise, NCC 1701-D

"WE'VE RECEIVED a Code Three distress call from the *U.S.S. Saladin.*"

Standing within the cowl of the bridge rail, First Officer William Riker faced the port side and spoke as the bridge suddenly boiled with activity. A terrible excitement came with Red Alert, a bewitching urge to run away or get on with it.

He wanted to deny that feeling or ignore it, but he couldn't. He hoped that bizarre anticipation didn't show in his face or in his straight posture as their commanding officer came down the bridge ramp toward him.

"Code Three," Captain Picard said. "That means they're under attack and being boarded."

Jean-Luc Picard's British enunciations did nothing to cool his words.

Will Riker towered over the captain but had never been able to upstage him. Picard was a subdued and steady man, compactly built, his head as nude as a Shaolin priest's, and he wore the black-and-maroon Starfleet uniform in a manner that seemed almost reluctant. He was a man of restricted movement who left his crew to discern only from his tone and his eyes what he was feeling.

They saw the silent wish for peace in his eyes. They saw it every day as he entered the bridge, and sometimes his wish was granted, but not today.

Code Three was a rare broadcast, a spindle of disaster drilling into the skull of every Starfleet officer, because it signified not just simple disaster but *inflicted* disaster.

Being boarded . . . a starship being boarded.

What would have to be done to a Federation starship, a Starfleet armed vessel, to effect a hostile boarding? Who had the power and cunning to get so far?

The turbolift door panels opened behind the horseshoe bridge rail, and Commander Data strode passively down the ramp and took his position at the operations control station on the forward command deck.

Picard held his breath until Data was seated. For some reason he took unexpected solace in the android's presence there. Likely it had something to do with the Code Three.

Then he looked at Riker.

Riker understood both the pause and the look. "We haven't been able to raise them since the initial call," he said. Then he, too, turned, this time to the upper deck and the Klingon officer manning the security and weapons station.

"We are nearing their coordinates," Lieutenant Worf rumbled.

"Raise shields," Riker told him, and turned forward again. "Prepare to go to impulse power."

As the ensign at the conn complied with the impulse preparation, Riker hesitated, seemed to think he might have compromised the captain's presence.

But Picard simply gazed at the great forward screen that showed them the oncoming spacescape, not concerned at the moment with making the ship move this way or that. He stood beside Riker and let his first officer be that extension of his command.

"Any other vessels in the area?" he asked.

"No, sir," Data answered. "Sensors show only the *Saladin*."

"Bring us out of warp," the captain said. "Put the *Saladin* on the screen."

Jean-Luc Picard watched as his crew played their panels like musical instruments, and there was even a certain computeristic music chirping about the wide earth-toned bridge. Only their black to-the-body uniforms and maroon, teal, or gold chest panels and sleeves provided any eruption from the sedate fawn colors of the bridge. Those colors certainly made duty crew assignments easy to spot.

The screen shifted a few times, far-reaching sensors struggling to bring in the images collected from extreme range. A moment later a pale image formed, then took sharp lines.

A Nebula-class Federation ship, obviously adrift, pocked with scorch marks . . . but the hull was intact.

The sight sucked the blood from those who lived on ships and depended upon them, spent the bulk of their time tending them, coddling them, mending them.

Attacked, boarded—and the hull still uncompromised?

From behind, Worf scanned his panel. "Their warp engines have been damaged, and defensive systems are off-line," he said, sounding puzzled, "but they still have main power . . . and there is no major structural damage."

A thousand questions pumped the captain's heart, stabbed at his mind, and he suddenly wanted answers to them all. He couldn't demand answers out of the air, nor could he squeeze them out of his crew, and he knew they were working as quickly as anyone could. They wanted answers too.

"Captain," Data interrupted.

Everyone looked at him, even crewmen who weren't supposed to look away from their work.

Android or not, Data felt the half dozen eyes on him, and he looked up.

"Sensors show no life aboard the *Saladin,*" he told them.

Picard glared forward, hoping in the depths of his heart to stare away those words, but again his shocked first officer spoke for them both.

"None?" Riker gasped.

Before them, Data's manufactured calmness was damning.

"No, sir," he said. "They are all dead."

Chapter Three

U.S.S. Saladin

COMMANDER RIKER got to the bridge first. That was their rendezvous point.

He got there, and his stomach turned.

The pulse point of the ship was nothing but a puddle of bodies.

Dead, bloody shells of Starfleet crew members of all kinds and sizes, all talents, all senses, armed and unarmed, littered the bridge decks. They'd fought, and they'd lost.

Beneath flickering backup lights and cloaked in a haze of battle smoke as it slowly cleared, *Saladin* Captain Harlock and his command crew lay where they'd been driven down. They had obviously fought hard, but only the security chief had been armed. The bridge walls were scarred with his phaser shots.

In spite of the effort, demolished bodies were draped over the helm, the rail, each other.

The security chief had gone down first and landed on top of his phaser. Gone down trying to do his job, getting in the first shot.

As Riker stepped among the bodies, he saw that the carpet was streaked with burns and smelled of smoke and death. He wished somebody else from the away team would come up here. Walking the dim bridge was akin to prowling a tomb, and he didn't like it. He'd stayed out of archaeology for a reason. He didn't want to spend his career unwrapping mummies, and now here he was, counting victims.

He bent over Captain Harlock's body and applied a little muscle to turning him over.

The captain almost broke in half at the pelvis.

Riker jumped back a step and winced. Allowed to flow, Harlock's blood drained slowly onto the carpet beneath Riker's boots.

Starting to clot. Hadn't been very long, though.

Where was the rest of the away team? He battled down a strong urge to call them. He knew perfectly well they weren't reporting in for good reason.

Because the words were ugly and the smell came with them.

He flinched when the turbolift doors gasped open, and before he even turned, it dawned on him just how much of the ship itself was still working. Lifts, doors, panels, internal and external systems . . .

It *was* all still working. A ship that had just been attacked and taken?

Why was it even still here?

He stepped gratefully away from Captain Harlock's remains and joined Engineer Geordi La Forge before the young man had to step down and defile the carpet and what soaked it.

La Forge's face, normally a nice healthy cocoa brown, was almost gray.

"Geordi," Riker moaned, "this is awful."

La Forge leaned one hand on the navigational auxiliary panel and tried to draw a deep breath.

"They're all dead," he rasped. "The whole crew. All over the ship, all different situations. Some were fighting, some were sleeping. Sir, you won't believe it. The—the purposefulness of it. They've had their . . ." He stopped.

"Spines severed?" Riker glanced down at the captain's mutilated body.

La Forge looked past him, his VISOR collecting data and filtering it instantly back to him, telling him things about the slaughter that neither of them really wanted to know. Skeletal ruptures, blood loss, heat dissipation, muscular strain, cerebral violation—

And he suddenly looked away.

Riker wondered what the young officer could see through that appliance, what he could witness about Captain Harlock's death and the death of everybody else draped around them, but he decided not to ask. If La Forge saw anything that needed reporting, he'd find a way to say it.

Blood in the carpet did a lot of talking for itself.

"What about this ship?" Riker asked. "Did you find anything? What were the attackers after?"

La Forge swallowed, drew the other half of that breath he'd been trying to get, and shook his head.

"Whatever they wanted," he said, "it wasn't the ship."

Enterprise

Captain's Log, Stardate 46772.4:
   Commander Riker's away team has completed its survey of the *Saladin,* and they have returned to the *Enterprise.* But we still have no idea who attacked the *Saladin . . .* or why.

Captain Picard tried to keep the emotion out of his face as Riker and Lieutenant Commander La Forge flanked him on the bridge. The details about Harlock's death—there was always something truly horrible about a captain's death, and not just to another captain—were gruesome and more than a little confusing.

"We found bodies everywhere," Riker said with effort. "At duty stations, in corridors, near escape pods, even some lying in their own beds. It was like walking through a slaughterhouse."

Picard despised himself for having sent them to see what he should have seen. He felt shielded and eccentric for not having gone himself. Now they had to relive the horror on his behalf.

La Forge didn't look good at all.

"You said the ship itself was undamaged?" Picard asked him.

"That's right," the engineer forced himself to say. "The computer core is intact. No equipment is missing. In fact, with the exception of the defense systems, the ship's still fully operational."

"There had to be some motive for this." The captain knew his frustration was showing. "Some reason to board a Federation starship and kill its crew . . ."

He knew he was stating the obvious, but somehow they all needed to hear these things, these unthinkable phrases, before they could pass over them and reach for answers. He had to get them to that point, and he had to get himself to it.

"Maybe killing the crew *was* the motive," Riker said. "Those people were killing methodically, efficiently, with very few wasted shots, and the attackers did it in less than fifteen minutes. They wanted to kill every single person aboard that ship . . . and they did."

Picard scowled. "Even terrorist raids have some rationale behind them. If we can determine who did this, we might also learn why."

"Captain," Worf's deep voice cut through like a foghorn. "We are receiving a distress call from the outpost on Ohniaka Three. They are under attack."

Picard swung around. "Red Alert. Set course for Ohniaka system and engage maximum warp." As the alert signal whooped through the ship, he thought aloud, "Ohniaka Three . . . There's no strategic value to that outpost. Isn't there any more information?"

Lieutenant Worf heard his captain's request. He worked, then worked some more. His dark face and ridged brow were panels of controlled fury. He looked as if he might rip the controls off and twist the ship's throat until he got his answers.

He didn't get them. Picard could see that he didn't like that.

And Worf obviously didn't like saying what he had to say either.

"I have lost contact with them, sir."

"We are entering the Ohniaka system."

Data's voice was steady enough to thread a needle.

Good thing, because everyone else was twisted tight.

"Bring us out of warp," Picard said to the ensign at the helm.

"Sensors detect one ship orbiting the third planet," Worf boomed from behind the command center. "Configuration does not match any in our records."

"Shields up," Riker barked. "Lock phasers on target. Stand by photon torpedoes."

Picard eyed the viewscreen, a distant view of the system they were approaching. "Hail the ship, Mr. Worf."

Worf worked with audible aggravation, then said, "No response."

"Put them on screen."

An optical appeared almost instantly as the sensors reached into the impossible distance and grabbed for manufactured solidity.

An alien vessel. Unfamiliar—the first alarm. It bore no markings, no decorations . . . and yet a haze of menace hung about its design.

Ridiculous, Picard thought. But he let himself feel menaced nonetheless. A little compulsive suspicion could be healthy at times.

"Information, Mr. Data?" he prodded.

"Sir, I am unable to scan the interior of the alien ship, but it does not appear to be attacking the outpost at this time."

Riker stood up, uneasy, the haze of what he had seen on *Saladin* still clinging to his expression. "They might have attacked before we got here."

Calmly Picard countered him with a gently warning tone. "Or they simply might be another victim. Data, what about the outpost on the surface?"

The android's hands played over his console, then again, even longer.

"There is a great deal of electromagnetic interference. I am unable to determine whether any lifeforms are still living on the surface."

Picard pressed his lips tight and drew a gust of bottled rage. Nothing about this was going to cooperate. Every step insisted upon being a risk. And he was going to have to do it again—send others where he wanted to go himself.

His neck almost twisted off, but he forced himself to nod at Riker.

At least he didn't have to say anything.

Riker lunged for the ramp. "Data, Worf! You're with me."

Federation Science Division Outpost, Ohniaka Three

William Riker stood stiffly as the transporter room dissolved around him, fizzled to lights, and almost immediately collected again into other colors and shapes. A ceiling, walls, computer desks—corpses, corpses, corpses.

He felt completely alone again, this crawling aloneness that involved other faces, but faces that only stared, and other bodies, but with no warmth. Suddenly he was glad he hadn't brought Geordi this time.

Beside him, Worf and Data were already scanning with their tricorders, analyzing the surroundings. Behind them, Security Ensign Corelki was shaking off the shock of what lay all around them.

Riker empathized with the disbelief in their eyes.

Everybody was heavily armed, but that didn't make him feel much better either.

Just like the Saladin, he thought.

Starfleet personnel, dead, dumped all around them like so much laundry.

Typical outpost, nothing special, except to the next of kin—a few scorch marks here and there, but no appreciable damage, not even a good gash in the wall to pretend interest in. Wishing for more damage, Riker found he had nothing to look at but the bodies.

"These wounds," Worf said critically as he waved his tricorder near a corpse, "were caused by a forced-plasma beam similar to the beam from a Ferengi hand phaser."

"This seems too brutal for the Ferengi," Riker responded. He turned to Data. "Can you detect survivors?"

Data paced slowly, watching the screen on his tricorder. "The electromagnetic interference is still making it difficult to get precise sensor readings."

Riker ignored him. "How many people were assigned to this outpost?"

"Two hundred seventy-four," Worf supplied instantly.

His blood running cold as he added up how many dozen in two hundred seventy-four, Riker sighed. "All right, we'll have to go from room to room. Maybe this time we'll find some survivors. Worf, you and Corelki start searching the north wing. We'll search the south wing."

"Aye, sir."

Worf was a big, *big* entity, and he was a Klingon, but even he was not so big and not so fearless that he didn't pull his phaser and aim it outward before taking one step outside the area.

The door to the north wing slid open as though laughing at them. No damage.

Riker watched as Worf and the security ensign disappeared into the depths of the science station, and the door closed again.

Not a good feeling at all. A brutal choice between

getting here too late and still being in the middle of lurking trouble. He didn't know which he would have chosen if he'd been given a choice.

He waved his own phaser at the other door, then glanced at Data, but the ship's second officer was already trying to operate the panel.

"The mechanism appears to be jammed," Data said as he tampered with the door-panel access. "I will attempt to bypass the main system."

Thanks for telling me, Riker thought bitterly. *Get us in there so we can confirm the body count. Maybe I could bypass the next ten minutes.*

"There's not much damage," he muttered. "Doesn't look like they were interested in the station . . . just the people."

Riker came from a very orderly world. Starfleet was orderly, Captain Picard's ship was orderly, things were quiet and stable, and most questions were answered right away. He could tackle a problem if he could see what it was. They all could. That was the way they were trained.

So where was the goddamn problem? Why wouldn't it show its face?

"I have bypassed the primary system," Data informed him. He might have been fishing for permission, even though he already knew the answer.

No, Riker thought. *I'm imagining that. I'm expecting him to act like a human. Subtle. Data's just not subtle.*

He turned, as did the others with him, to the door to the south wing. They took a step toward it, the way steps are taken toward getting unpleasantness over with.

But as the door slid open, unpleasantness drafted a new appearance. Familiar and horrible, it was the face of mechanization gone mad. A face of dead humanity confiscated and forced to keep living, as though one of these corpses had been stood up, fitted with tubes, life support, and body armor, and propped against a wall with its eyes open.

Borg . . . Borg . . . Borg!

Riker's mind clanged with a word that was its own warning, and he wished he'd never seen one before, but he had. Real close up.

And this one was real close too.

Before he could move, before anyone, even Data, could move, the Borg was firing its built-in weaponry. Bolts of energy cut across the room.

As he and Data fired wildly and dived for cover, Will Riker realized through his astonishment that they'd just found the goddamn problem.

Chapter Four

Enterprise

"BATTLE STATIONS! Full shields!"

Jean-Luc Picard's deep voice turned corrosive and his small eyes, fractious. On the giant forward screen, the alien ship had come to life in a most malevolent manner and was spitting poison at them like some kind of veldt adder.

"Evasive maneuvers, Ensign!" he called to the helm. "Return fire!"

The painfully obvious orders were also painfully necessary. No one but the senior bridge command could issue either of those instructions.

Again venom spit, malicious streaks of constricted energy, and slammed the starship square in the forward shields—a strike for the heart.

There was no caginess about it, no trick, no dodging or strategy. The other ship stood toe-to-toe and battered at them. Just an infuriating direct hard hit, the kind delivered by a bully who knew his own strength. The other ship didn't even make any attempt to dodge the starship's return fire.

"Shields are down to eighty percent!" Geordi called from his station. "Compensating with auxiliary power—"

He was cut off as the ship was hit again and canted to starboard before recovering.

Picard clung to his command lounge. "Who are they? No one in this sector bears any malice toward the Federation! Analyze those beams—get some kind of correlation out of the computer. Perhaps we can use it to identify them. And someone attempt to make contact with the away team!"

Ohniaka Station

Borg, Borg, Borg!

With his brain shouting that single chilling word at him, Riker had to plow through shock and disbelief and fire back as more of the mindless automated devils, so bitterly familiar to him, came charging into the research area.

This was the Federation's recurring nightmare, and certainly the *Enterprise*'s. Added to the long history of firsts attributed to the starships called *Enterprise* was the first encounter with the nation of Borg, partly biological, partly robotic beings, run by a single control center, devoid of passion or pain, blunted of any emotion, relentless to the extreme. Nightmare, yes.

Cybernetics gone mad. Mutation of machine and being. Their bluish faces helmeted with armor, coiled with tubing, half covered by audio- and visual-enhancement mechanisms, their forms coated with black body armor and bionic generator components. Ugly. Just ugly.

Riker and Data were behind desks, already cornered and driven down to defense. His heart slammed against his breastbone. He hadn't gotten a whole breath yet, and he needed one. At least Data would remain unexcited. That gave the two of them an extra measure of advantage.

And they needed it. The Borg semi-robots fired relentlessly, shot after shot, filling the room with the snapping crackle of energy bolts. Riker got precious few opportunities to fire back without having his beard singed.

This didn't make sense. He should have been able to get a clear shot, should have been able to take the Borgs' heads off one by one in a situation like this. They were all worker bees, dull-witted drones willing to die for the swarm, with no sense of personal salvation.

So why were they hiding and ducking and dodging? Why were their faces twisted with wrath. These were mutated still further, past the stage of mindlessness and into something else. Fury.

Am I imagining this? Did they catch me just a little too much by surprise?

He lunged from his hiding place, rolled, and landed behind a steel shipping crate, using Data's shots as cover, and he snatched from those few seconds one good look at the Borg.

No, he wasn't imagining. These Borg weren't acting like the ones he had seen before. They were moving fast—fast! They were hiding, avoiding being shot, and their eyes were crimped with rage and purpose.

How many were there? He couldn't even tell. One simple strategical fact and he couldn't get it. The two of them would drain their phasers in seconds against these mutated cyborgs.

The north wing door broke open, and Worf and his ensign charged back in, firing as they hit the threshold, but the quick-moving Borg drove them to cover immediately. There wasn't even an instant of advantage. The Starfleet crew was still outgunned, outnumbered, but Riker took the chance that the Borg might be distracted by Worf and the guard.

Gritting his teeth, ready to be scorched into a fizzle himself, he dodged from his cover long enough to get out one shot at the nearest Borg—and made it! His phaser shot seared across the Borg's throat and cut its life support, then cauterized the tubing beyond repair.

The monster went down behind a console.

One of the other Borg stopped firing and tried to

catch the one that went down, but there wasn't anything to be done.

That was not surprising in a battle like this. The surprise came when the Borg looked up from his comrade's body, its face distorted with anger.

"You have killed Torsus!" it accused. "I will make you suffer for this!"

Riker stared. Behind him, Worf and Corelki paused in their hiding places, and even Data, just a few feet away, seemed confused.

A second Borg peeked from its own hiding place and its glare connected with Worf, then with Riker. "Biological organism Klingon," it said, "Biological organism human, I will destroy you."

Not just information but a bald threat. A promise.

The same Borg found Data among the corpses and furnishings and continued, "Artificial life-form: Starfleet. Rank: lieutenant commander. Name: Data."

Riker held very still and willed Data to do the same, to keep from responding to what seemed more like a beckoning than an analysis.

The Borg looked at each other as though sending silent messages. What were they saying to each other now that they knew whom they were fighting?

How could they know Data's name?

Riker was about to yell his question out when one of the Borg leaped, its face flushed nearly purple with unmistakable rage.

Hearing a distinct "uh-oh" go off in his head,

Riker pushed off and dodged for the back of the room, trying to get closer to Worf and Corelki so that they could make a stand, combine their fire, try something wild. Worf had the quickness to cover him with nearly constant phaser shots.

A ghastly shriek filled the room—a scream, a howl—and in the middle of his run Riker instinctively turned.

The Borg were rushing them! Physically attacking like Celts charging from the Highlands, plunging down on them.

Riker took several blows before he could even see which Borg was hitting him. The breath was crushed from his body, and striking back was nothing more than his training reacting for him. In his blurred peripheral vision he saw Data dispatch a Borg with one kick, but another Borg screamed, shrieked, blew in like a storm wind, and slammed Data backward against a wall so hard that the wall gave way.

The Borg weren't firing their weapons—they were fighting, wrestling! Trying to kill with their hands!

This is crazy! It's impossible! Where's their pattern? Where's the predictability!

Riker wanted to get a breath and shout something, anything, to encourage his team, but the Borg were on him, punching, kicking, teeth gritted, humanoid eyes shrewish as they pummeled him. Over in the corner, two more of them were pummeling Worf, and even with his Klingon fury boiling and that inhuman strength coming to bear, Worf was losing.

Taking the Borg's blows on his arms and doing everything he could to protect his vital organs, Riker tried to back himself against a support beam and maybe get one arm down. If he could just touch his communication badge, just send one split-second message through to the ship, the transporter could home in on their drumming heartbeats and pull them out of this.

If he could just get a hand down there without getting his head crushed . . .

Losing. We're losing. . . . We'll be like these others, draped over the desks, torn in half. . . .

"Stop it!"

Riker flinched under the blows he was taking. Had he shouted? That voice hadn't been Worf's deep boom.

The two Borg who were on him broke away suddenly, and he found himself sagging, staring.

"Stop it!"

He focused on the sound, and found it.

Data? The shimmering android face, normally a perfect impassive etching, was twisted with frenzy, and there was acid in the golden eyes. Data snarled, then seized two handfuls of cybernetic coils and hoisted one of the Borg full into the air and right over his head.

"Stop it!" he shrieked again and flung the Borg against a console.

The console collapsed under the great stress, and the Borg went down, crumpled.

31

A chance, a fleeting chance. Now Data would turn on another Borg and cut their numbers by another . . .

Riker stared, his lungs begging for air, and his flash of hope soured.

Data didn't turn on another Borg. He grabbed at the throat of the same Borg, the one who was already down.

He hauled the Borg up and slammed it against a wall and growled in its face. "Stop it!"

Data was roaring mad and showing it.

"Stop it! Stop it! Stop it!" With every word, Data again slammed the Borg into the wall. His expression was virulent, his face jaundiced and rabid.

Riker wanted to pull him back, but he knew he didn't have the strength. Nobody had that kind of strength. And the desire to stop him was not very strong. He too was taking each blow as satisfaction.

But it was all over in a wink, before he could even find his legs and think about using them.

The demolished victim slumped to the floor at Data's feet.

As though waking from a dream, Data blinked downward. He seemed confused. The violence drained from his face, leaving only a void quickly filling with question.

The other cyborgs, now acting like the single-unit extensions Riker had expected at first, stepped back from their attacks, let their eyes go blank, and simply dematerialized.

Gone, as suddenly as they'd appeared.

"Captain, the alien ship is breaking orbit!"

Geordi La Forge didn't mean to raise his voice, but he did so all the time and just hoped the captain might be used to it by now. Starfleet officers were supposed to be serene and calm and never raise their voices, but today he'd just have to live with not being perfect.

Maybe it was a twinge of guilt. Maybe he wanted to be down there with the away team, doing the other half of what he and Riker had started.

"Set an intercept course," Picard was saying to the helm ensign. Then, to Tactical, he added, "Continue firing. Transfer auxiliary power to shields."

Geordi leaped to action at his Engineering console on the aft bridge. Now he had something to do. The hum of the great starship's enormous engines and unthinkable bottled power came up through his legs as the big ship turned and surged to full impulse.

The brilliance of impulse power had been overshadowed by the discovery of hyperlight, but at times like this he could feel the miracle of sublight— power compounding on itself while the starship was still a part of nature, still moving at less than the speed of light. Maneuverability was at its peak, the stars were clear and defiant in the sky, the starship's pure muscle flexed.

Would've been pretty, had it not been for that ship out there.

He turned to look at the forward screen. Through his VISOR he saw the heat radiated from his shipmates, saw that they were all tense, and on the screen he saw the spectral representations of stars on the star field, and power emanations from that ship.

And he saw the thing open up.

Staring like an idiot, he stumbled forward until the tactical station stopped him. A *light* . . . opened up. A big hole in the material of open space, shining in their eyes.

The enemy ship looped into the portal, plunged deep inside, and the thing closed up again.

Everybody stared, even Captain Picard.

"Mr. La Forge?" the captain asked.

"They're gone, sir," Geordi uttered. "Our sensors indicate there was some kind of subspace distortion just before they disappeared. I'll have to study these readings before I can get more specific."

They also saw that this wasn't just a dime-store deep-space energy portal. This one had opened up on purpose, under somebody's control.

This was an escape hatch.

The captain fixed an accusative scowl upon the silent vista of space.

"Take us back to Ohniaka Three."

Which side of the looking glass am I on today?

Will Riker pushed himself shakily to his full height. He was breathing like a bellows, and his legs shook under him so violently that he had to concentrate in order to take a step. He looked at Worf.

The Klingon was across the room, still crouched in attack stance as though he didn't believe the retreat either. He was ready to pounce, but willing to take Riker's lead.

So . . . lead.

Riker pushed himself forward—yes, he still had his knees—and moved toward Data. Worf moved forward too, and they converged on their enigmatic crewmate.

If Data could somehow have been spontaneously violent, then now he could be spontaneously shocked. His normally placid face shimmered with spent energy, and he seemed dazed, puzzled, unsure of his own memory of the past moments' vulgarities.

That uncertainty in itself was unsettling to see. Data had memory banks, not a memory, and he shouldn't have that just-awakening look in his eyes, wondering if he'd really just pulverized an entity that was no less living than he was.

Then what were they seeing?

Riker shoved down his apprehension and moved closer.

"Data?" he began gently. "Data, are you all right?"

"Yes, sir," Data answered.

Too quickly.

If he meant he hadn't had an arm pulled off, then he *was* all right. But how was he . . . inside?

"What happened?" Riker prodded.

Data gazed downward, as though seeking his momentary rage the way a curious child might turn over a dead hornet and look for the stinger.

He blinked again, then looked up. Stiffly he turned to Riker and Worf and picked through corruption in search of objectivity.

"I got angry," he said.

Chapter Five

Enterprise, Sickbay

SHIP'S COUNSELOR DEANNA TROI felt her stomach automatically tighten as she entered sickbay.

That feeling didn't make any sense, but it always happened to her as she came into this area. Possibly it was a reaction to the faint medicinal smell that never went away, or perhaps it was her awareness that this was where people ended up when they were in real trouble.

In her mind she knew that sickbay was just another lab, a place where problems could be solved and discoveries made, but that didn't help her stomach.

She allowed herself a crooked smile. If others had this feeling, it would be Deanna's job to come up with a soft clinical explanation and send them on their way somewhat purged.

Sickbay was very quiet.

Where was everyone?

This place was worse when it was silent than when it was bustling with wounded or ill crewmen.

Oh, what an unforgivable thought, she scolded herself, and pushed on into the inner examining rooms.

"Beverly?" she called. "Are you in here?"

From the senior medical officer's desk area, a voice called back. "Yes, Deanna, I'm in here. Thinking about yarn."

What an elegant voice their senior surgeon had. *If I had a voice like that, I'd be on the stage.*

"Yarn?" Deanna murmured, and frowned.

Everyone always told Deanna she was beautiful, a perfect combination of Grecian black eyes, tumbling black curls, and ivory skin, and people used exotic terms when they wanted to give her a complement, but when she herself thought of beauty, she thought of Beverly Crusher.

Beverly possessed a certain balance and symmetry that Deanna envied in the dark hours of her day, the cheekbones and glowing copper hair of some lingering Irish queen, and a lurking mischievousness that rarely showed itself but that definitely lurked behind her azure eyes.

And here they were, both scientists instead of painters' models.

Deanna shook her head, smiled again, and strode through sickbay into the office.

Beverly was sitting behind her desk, leaning back, with her blue medical smock flopping over the arms of the chair at her sides. Her hair was uncombed and still looked good—certainly a Celtic magic trick Deanna had never mastered—and a devilish half grin pulled at the doctor's cheeks.

"Did you say 'yarn'?" Deanna asked. "You mean, like a tall story?"

"No," the doctor said. "I mean like thread. Yarn. The long thin twisted material sweaters are knitted from. I was thinking of colors of yarn and all those pretty names the manufacturers give them. You know . . . seafoam green and periwinkle blue, slate black, Vulcan red, Bordeaux, roccelline, strawberry, Quaker gray . . ."

"Oh," Deanna responded. "Where is everyone?"

"It's lunchtime. Goldenrod, Mars orange, shamrock—"

"Lunch? Aren't your interns and nurses on some kind of rotation?"

"Of course, but I don't care for rotation. I like them to be able to go to lunch together. Sit down. Talk to each other about things that don't involve touch pads and retrieval indicators. I like them to get to know each other."

Deanna sat down on the consultation couch and crossed her legs.

"Don't delude yourself," she warned. "They'll

talk about those things anyway. We're all obsessed
with our jobs. What if something happened and you
needed them for some medical emergency?"

"Deanna, they're only two decks away."

"That's true. Why were you thinking about
thread? You don't sew, do you?"

"No, and I don't knit either, but I'd like to learn
someday," the doctor said, rolling back again, and
the chair creaked under her.

"You should have that creak fixed."

"I like the creak. It's the chair's way of singing to
me."

"Oh . . . sorry."

Beverly ran a finger along her chin and gazed at the
ceiling. "Do you ever get the urge to do something
underhandedly female? Something completely vile
and one-sidedly womanish?"

Deanna switched her legs around to push a few
seconds by, and felt her smile twist up again. "Like
what?"

"Like having a quilting bee."

"A quilting what? Bee?"

"Every now and then I get an urge to go off to the
Ohio countryside and sit around a really big wooden
table with lots of splinters in it, and talk to a lot of
extremely plain women about gourd ladles and lye
soap while we stitch patches of fabric onto a big fat
quilt that looks like ten suns rising." She shifted her
gaze to Deanna and added, "How do you think I'd
look in black clothes with one of those little white
caps?"

Deanna laughed. "You'd look like a nun having naughty thoughts. You have an evil look about you, you know."

"Yes, I know that."

"Is that why you don't comb your hair? You don't like to look in the mirror?"

"Oh, low blow," the doctor hooted. "One for your side."

"Why don't you just go down to the holodeck and call up an Amish scenario? You could quilt your off hours away."

Beverly moved forward slightly, and the chair made a happy squawk.

"That's the problem. I could do anything I wanted on the holodeck, but I wouldn't *really* be doing it. It's the people, the conversation, the camaraderie. The holodeck never gets the people exactly right."

Leaning an elbow on her knee, Deanna watched the doctor's sedate face and that nefarious glitter behind those eyes. "That's right—you don't use the holodeck very often, do you?"

"Not anymore. It's irresistible at first, but that door has to open eventually. I swear I can just barely see the black and yellow grid just behind the mist of every scenario. What do you think? You want to start a quilting club with me? We can make rag rugs and everything."

"If you can find a rag on board," Deanna said with a shrug. "There might be a certain flaw about it. Don't you think the men will accuse us of being parochial?"

"Well, they can join if they want to." Beverly leaned forward again, braced both elbows on her desk, and lowered her head conspiratorially, as though she was planning a heist. "So? What do you say?"

Deanna stared at her, then laughed. "Why do I feel as though I've just joined a coven?"

The doctor only offered her a smile designed to be wicked.

"Riker to Medical."

"Ah, William the First. A prime target for a spell if ever I met one." Beverly winked, then straightened and tapped the comm badge. "Sickbay, Crusher."

"Doctor, can you and Counselor Troi join us, please, in the observation lounge? We think we've got a real problem."

"We'll be right there."

She stood up, towering over Troi.

Troi got up too, reluctantly, and managed not to giggle.

"Oh, they've got a problem," she said. "They've got us."

Captain's Log, Stardate 46982.1:
   Because of his unusual behavior on the planet surface, Commander Data has asked to be temporarily relieved of duty. Unfortunately, this means he will not be able to help us investigate a disturbing new change in the behavior of the Borg.

Observation Lounge

The quiet librariesque place offered only a gauze of peace to the officers seated around its table of wood and dark glass, a pretense they all knew wasn't real and wouldn't hold.

Riker clenched his hands under the table and took as much solace as he could get from the faces of his captain and his peers. Worf was here, so he knew anything he imagined from those looking-glass moments would be corrected if he got it wrong.

He was already knotted up from describing what had happened to them on Ohniaka Three, and talking about it hadn't been any easier or any more purging than going through it in the first place.

And he was embarrassed. He was a senior officer, supposedly able to deal with the unexpected at any turn. He'd done that before and come out all right, without this layer of ice under his skin that wouldn't go away.

But what he had seen on Ohniaka . . . left him cold in the bones.

Across the table, Deanna Troi and Dr. Beverly Crusher were an oasis of pleasantness for him.

He took all he could get.

"They were fast," he told them. "Aggressive . . . almost vicious. It was more like fighting Klingons than Borg. No offense," he added, with a glance at Worf.

"None taken," the giant of security rumbled.

"There was another difference. I don't think they

43

were part of the Borg collective. They acted more like individuals."

"What?" the captain said sharply.

But Riker wasn't inclined to back down from the captain's blunt question. "One of them referred to himself as 'I.'"

"That Borg," Worf added, "also showed concern for a fallen comrade and called him by name."

A frown crinkled Deanna's ivory brow. "The only Borg who ever had a name," she said, "was Hugh. And we gave it to him."

"Maybe Hugh has something to do with this change in their behavior," Beverly said.

The name rumbled through their collective memory. Hugh. A Borg who had entered their lives in a different way from any other of his violent kind. Who had ended up with a personality, asked them questions, wondered about himself.

Nothing an ordinary Borg could do. Just as Data could not possibly have a real emotion.

Could it be that there was something inside the biological part of a bionic being, Riker wondered, something that lingered of life, which could be awakened?

Evolution was a funny thing. Nobody really understood it.

The captain stood up.

Riker watched as the captain moved to the tall viewing ports and stared out into space. They knew his involvement with the Borg had been more deeply personal than any living being deserved.

Picard was one of a kind. The only human of his kind, just as Data was the only one of his kind, and Hugh one of his kind. Picard was a human who had been captured by the Borg but not treated like a prisoner. The Borg had used a different method. They had incorporated him into that mechanized swarm, forced him to give up his personhood, to do the bidding of the singular mind.

Later released again to his individual identity, stolen back from the thieves by his own people, Jean-Luc Picard now had to live with what he had done under the other identity.

A living, pulsing identity with the soul of a machine.

The tool of invasion. Of murder—slaughter—of his own people.

Not something any person with a conscience could easily accept.

Nor could they all simply ignore their involvement with Hugh, an innocent piece of the puzzle in whom they'd found a flicker of humanity.

"Hugh," Picard murmured, "whom we sent back to the Borg in the hope that he would have an impact on them, that he would change them." With his back still to them, he added, "And now it would seem that the Borg have changed."

He didn't turn. He stared out the viewport at the vastness of space. Dark implications orbited him as he stood in silence.

"Did they show any interest in assimilating you or your technology?" he asked.

Riker held his breath a moment, then realized for the ten thousandth time that the privileges of his rank also carried the responsibility of answering first. "They seemed more concerned with the death of their colleague and with destroying us. I didn't see anything that suggested they wanted to assimilate anyone."

Riker heard his own voice, his effort to maintain stability in his tone as he tried to sound casual and not accusatory, but he couldn't hang on to his own efforts as he watched guilt creep into his captain's demeanor.

The captain's voice was troubled. "The Borg's entire existence," he said, "was centered around the acquisition of technology and cultures. If that is no longer the case, then they must have a new objective. We have to find out what it is."

They were all afraid that they'd done this by proxy somehow, that their trickle of hope—Hugh—had turned out to be the cause of the horrors they'd witnessed.

"What about Data?" Beverly interrupted. "Do you have any idea what happened to him?"

Riker tore his perceptive gaze away from the captain and cleared his throat.

"Geordi's checking him out right now," he said. "I don't know what to make of his behavior, but for a moment, he certainly appeared to be angry."

That behind-the-looking-glass sensation again, for all of them this time.

The Borg with individuality, Data without control . . .

Still gazing out the portal with his back to them, the captain remained silent.

Empathy surged through Riker, but he knew there were some things a man had to go through alone. The captain had gone through his Borg experience alone, and they could do nothing for him when memories of that time came to chill his heart.

So Riker just watched him, and felt a little bad even to be doing that.

"Mr. Worf," the captain said, his voice somber, gruff, "from this moment on, we will maintain Security Condition Two. Have armed security officers posted on every deck, and give defense systems priority over everything but life support."

"Aye, sir," Worf responded.

"Number One, analyze our sensor readings of the Borg ship. Try to ascertain whether it's a vessel they constructed or an alien ship they captured. Then begin a study of this . . . subspace distortion they used to escape."

Riker nodded. "Aye, sir."

Now Picard turned.

His distinct features were stark and grim, his shoulders stiff, and his arms pinned to his sides. He didn't make eye contact with anyone.

"I'm going to contact Starfleet Command."

Engineering Deck

Thinking maybe he should open up an emergency ward, Geordi La Forge zapped and buzzed and plinked at the circuitry inside a very small panel with a very small tool. Things tended to be small when they were packed inside a human head.

Well, okay, not exactly human.

He just tended to want to think of Data that way. So he had a hard time thinking of Data's head as just another machine, in spite of the fact that he was looking at the blinking connections right now.

"Your positronic net checks out," he said. "Everything looks fine."

Maybe Dr. Crusher would give him something medical-looking to hang around his neck and a nice smock to wear.

"My internal diagnostics also found nothing wrong," Data responded blandly.

Geordi put the masking panel back on the side of Data's head and wondered how often ordinary people got to close up their friends' heads.

"I don't know what to say, Data. There's nothing here to indicate anything that would cause a behavioral anomaly."

"I agree," the android said. "Geordi . . . I believe I experienced my first emotion."

Holding his breath for a moment, Geordi put his tools down and turned toward what he had just heard.

"Data," he began, "no offense, but how would you

know an actual flash of anger from some kind of odd power surge?"

Data hesitated. If he could be disappointed, then he was. His voice was subdued, and he wasn't looking up.

"You are correct in that I have no frame of reference with which to positively confirm my hypothesis. In fact, I find myself unable to provide a verbal description of the experience. Perhaps you could describe what it feels like when *you* get angry. I could use your description as a standard by which to judge myself."

He pushed off the bench and looked at Geordi with his big yellow eyes.

Geordi shifted from foot to foot. Not exactly the kind of heart-to-heart talk friends had over hot chocolate. He could describe the inside of the warp engine, a nearly impossible science, but he couldn't describe the simple art of flying off the handle.

"Well . . . when I get angry . . . first I begin to feel . . . hostile."

"Could you describe feeling hostile?" Data whipped back.

"It's feeling . . . belligerent . . . combative."

"Could you describe feeling angry without referring to other feelings?"

Geordi struggled with that for a few seconds. It was a good question.

Not one that popped up every day.

"No," he sighed, "I guess not. I just . . . *feel* angry."

Data tilted his head. "That was my experience as well. I simply . . . *felt* angry."

"Let's say you're right," Geordi said, "that this was an emotion. How is that possible?"

"I do not know. Perhaps I have evolved to the point where emotions are within my reach. Perhaps I will have more emotions as time goes on."

Geordi smiled, shrugged, and started to put his equipment away.

"I hope you're right," he said. "I'd hate to think anger is all you're capable of feeling."

Captain's Log, Stardate 46984.6:
  No additional Borg attacks have been reported in the past two days. However, Starfleet has dispatched Admiral Nechayev to take command in this sector in preparation for a possible Borg invasion. Admiral Nechayev has arrived aboard the *Starship Gorkon,* which is running abeam of the *Enterprise* at this moment.

Captain Picard wanted to go in any direction other than the one he was committed to. No matter how he grasped for steady emotions, he couldn't be cool regarding the Borg. These creatures had sucked him into their virulent culture and used him against his own people.

He couldn't bury that memory. He couldn't bury a fear so cloying or a guilt so portentous.

Nor could he keep those debilitating sensations from his eyes as he gazed at Admiral Nechayev while she ticked off the plans for the immediate future. Each detail was a nail in Picard's heart.

"There will be fifteen starships in this sector by the

day after tomorrow," the admiral explained. "The *Gorkon* will be my flagship. You'll have command of Task Force Three, consisting of the *Enterprise,* the *Crazy Horse,* and the *Agamemnon.*"

Picard forced his voice through his constricted throat and battled to sound utterly controlled. He knew he wasn't pulling it off as well as the admiral was.

"Understood," he said.

Nechayev was forcing blandness, though neither of them would have admitted what they were holding in. Her straw-blond hair in that piled-up, uncomfortable-looking style did little to assist the pointy Slavic features or to add warmth or kindness to her eyes. She was painfully efficient and working hard to simply say what she had to say.

"Captain," she spoke evenly, "I've read the report you submitted to Admiral Brooks last year regarding the Borg you called Hugh, and I've been trying to figure out why you let him go."

Nechayev allowed for an awkward pause. Neither of them appreciated the artwork of such a moment in history. They both knew, from two unfortunate angles, of Picard's intimate involvement in the other Borg encounters, and both recognized the irony of his involvement yet again.

"I thought I made my reasons clear," Picard said to her.

The admiral paused, glanced downward for a moment, then looked up again.

She was going to talk about this whether he wanted to or not. He could see that in her face and he tensed for the obligatory not-your-faults, all the things he would tell someone if it had happened to a member of his crew rather than to him.

Only when she spoke her first phrase did he realize he was reading her wrong and she wasn't going to give him the senior-officer buffer he dreaded, but instead the candor he dreaded more.

"As I understand it," she said, "you found a single Borg at a crash site, brought it aboard the *Enterprise,* studied it, analyzed it, and eventually found a way to send it back to the Borg with a program that would destroy the entire collective once and for all."

He didn't want her here, didn't want to have to endure this conversation face to face, yet he was enduring it anyway. She had been brought here by the fabulous magic of light speed, and this was the miracle of technology to which it seemed at times that they were all slaves.

Picard knew what it was to be a slave. He remembered the flashes of identity that had come like needles through the blockheaded persona the Borg had forced upon him. *Locutus . . . my name is Locutus. . . .*

I am Picard, starship captain, and you cannot use me again. I will not be used again.

Humiliation boiled within him. Somehow he was responsible for anything these creatures did, every innocent life snuffed out in their path.

He didn't want to be scolded.

"But instead," Nechayev said, pressing on, "you nursed the Borg back to health, treated it like a guest, gave it a name, and then sent it home. Why?"

Picard glared back at her. Hugh. Locutus. Painful details. Things that had happened already but refused to be relegated to the past.

The Borg had done to him what he and his officers had done to Hugh: captured him, indoctrinated him, and released him into an enemy horde for a singular purpose.

But he could match hard for hard, and this was as good a time as any.

"Once Hugh was separated from the Borg collective, he began to grow and evolve into something more than just an automaton. He was a person. When that happened, I had no choice but to respect his rights as an individual—"

"Of course you had a choice," Nechayev interrupted. "You could've taken the opportunity to rid the Federation of a mortal enemy, one that has killed tens of thousands of innocent people and which may kill even more."

"No one is more aware of the danger than I am. But I am also bound by my oath and my conscience to uphold certain principles. And I will not sacrifice them in order to—"

"Your priority is to safeguard the lives of Federation citizens, not to wrestle with your conscience," Nechayev parried. "Now I want to make it clear that if you have a similar opportunity in the future, an opportunity to destroy the Borg, you are under orders to take advantage of it. Is that understood?"

Picard gave himself a moment to breathe. He wasn't being scolded—exactly.

He was being warned. Ordered. No blurred lines today.

Not very deep down he knew she was right.

He and Hugh. They were both infiltrators. Brainwashed pawns. And he would never have thought it possible of himself.

Gathering his ravaged pride and the sense of personal worth that had been shredded by the Borg, Picard squared his shoulders and simply said, "Yes, Admiral."

He knew Nechayev was as relieved as he himself when she was able to get up and leave. She would be relieved to get back on the *Gorkon,* and she would be relieved to take her ship away.

If only either of them could be relieved about anything else today.

"In the past six hours, I have attempted to elicit an emotional response by subjecting myself to various stimuli. I have listened to several operas known to be uplifting, I watched three holodeck programs designed to be humorous, and I made several attempts to induce sexual desire by subjecting myself to erotic imagery."

Deanna Troi listened as Commander Data ticked off his efforts to get a feeling out of himself, and thought back on her training in field psychology to see if any of her professors had anticipated anything like this session.

She was sitting here talking to an android, listening to his attempts to induce reactions in himself, knowing that he expected her to do the impossible: analyze the psychological reactions of a being who wasn't supposed to have any.

Who wasn't *able* to have any. Whose apparent reactions until now had been nothing more than mimicry of what he saw around him. That was the difference. Living beings could experience new feelings. Androids could only imitate other people's feelings.

Or so everyone had thought, until now.

She suspected that Data was just talking to her because that was what everybody else did.

But that was part of the problem—Data trying to be more human by *mimicking* humanity. He had it all backwards.

Including today.

"What happened?" she asked him.

"Nothing," Data said.

She crossed her legs, bent forward, and tried to force herself not to treat him like an android. After all, that definitely wasn't why he came to her.

"I'm curious. Why have you ignored the one emotion you've already experienced? Why haven't you tried to make yourself angry again?"

Data's soft voice had no more tension in it than ever, but his eyes were somehow troubled.

"Anger is a negative emotion," he said. "I wanted to concentrate on something more positive."

"Feelings aren't positive or negative, Data," Deanna said. She also had to fight her urge to treat him like a child, even though in many ways he was. "It's what we *do* with those feelings that becomes good or bad. For example, feeling angry about an injustice could actually lead someone to take a positive action to correct that injustice."

"But my study of humanity indicates that some emotions are harmful, such as prejudice, hatred, sadistic urges . . . Should I not avoid those feelings if possible?"

Deanna leaned back and sighed. Such innocence. She would have framed him, if she could have, to preserve him in his kindhearted efficiency. He was searching for emotion, for some semblance of humanness in himself, but she couldn't help feeling that something would be lost if he ever found it. His effort alone was so endearing. Wasn't that an emotion too?

"Those are very strong emotions," she agreed, "and you're right. Very little good can come out of them. But I don't think an exploration of anger necessarily leads to feelings of hate or malice."

Was that adequate? She waited and watched him.

"But what if it does, Counselor?" he asked. "What if I find that those are the only emotions I am capable of experiencing? Will that make me a bad person?"

Deanna felt herself begin to smile, but a part of her wanted to cry. Data wasn't the average patient or client, or whatever these searching individuals were who came to solicit her opinion of their mental states. He would remember everything she said, analyze her words, her expressions, judge himself against them unforgivingly.

That, too, was an emotion, she realized: Data had trouble forgiving himself.

She could tell him how rare and wonderful she thought he was, but he wouldn't understand it. If she wasn't analytical, he wouldn't know what she meant.

She smiled gently at him.

"Data, let me say something from a personal standpoint," she offered. "We've served a long time together, and I've gotten to know you pretty well. I have to believe that if you ever do become human . . . you won't become a bad one."

The android grew quiet.

Her words warmed the room but somehow failed to warm Data. He still seemed troubled.

"There is another reason why I am concerned," he said finally. "When I was fighting the Borg, I felt angry, but when I think back on the incident, I experience a different sensation. It is not the same as anger, but I think it might be an emotion."

"Perhaps it's guilt," Deanna said. "It would be a very natural response to feel remorse about killing someone."

Data looked up at her in a most odd way, a way that sent a shiver down her arms. When he spoke again, his words threw Deanna's glimmer of hope into the trash.

"I do not believe it is guilt, Counselor," he admitted. "I believe it is pleasure."

Chapter Six

"RED ALERT! All hands to battle stations!"

Riker turned away from Worf at the tactical station and snapped at the conn officer, "Lay in a course and engage at warp nine!"

Crew members emerged from the lifts around the bridge and flew to their stations. Captain Picard entered from the ready room, and only that showed Riker how few seconds had gone by since the emergency erupted.

Data appeared on the aft bridge and came forward to the Ops position. Riker ignored him and went straight to the captain.

"We have a distress call from the New Berlin colony. They're under attack."

Picard nodded at him coldly, stepped past him, and spoke to Data.

"What's our ETA?"

Data tapped the control surface of his display panel. "At present speed, we will arrive in fifteen minutes, thirty seconds."

The captain gestured back to Worf. "Contact the *Crazy Horse* and the *Agamemnon*. Tell them to stand by in case we—"

"Incoming message, Captain," Worf broke in. "It's the New Berlin colony."

Riker felt his muscles knot. Ready for another body count. He didn't want to go through that again.

And he didn't want the captain to go through it.

"They are canceling their distress call," Worf said. He scowled at his equipment, then huffed in disapproval. "A Ferengi trading ship entered their system and someone panicked . . . again."

With a bitter sigh, Riker grumbled, "That's the third time today. Conn, reduce speed to warp six and bring us back to our patrol route."

He would've waited for the captain to give the obvious order himself, but that would've been dangerous.

Captain Picard was horn-mad, and they could all see it. He didn't want to have to issue common orders, and it was Riker's job to make sure he didn't have to.

Riker *hoped,* at least.

The captain held his temper as though reining in a

foaming horse. His voice had an underlying roar about it.

"Mr. Worf, stand down from Red Alert. Acknowledge the signal from New Berlin and then transmit a copy of Starfleet's recognition protocols, and tell them to read it this time."

"Aye, sir."

Riker watched the captain escape into his ready room.

They all did.

Captain's Log, Supplemental:
   We have been on patrol for seventeen hours, and there are still no reports of any further Borg activity. But tensions continue to run high on the colonies and outposts in this sector.

Picard's voice was brusque, his manner choppy, caged.

Will Riker wasn't even inside the ready room yet, but he could already hear—or maybe just sense— the captain making that log entry. Slow words, sluggish, half his mind on something else . . .

He hesitated a moment, then buzzed.

Seconds twisted away. Riker shifted back and forth and almost left.

"Come," the captain's voice caught him just in time.

And the first officer still almost didn't go in, but now it was too late.

The captain was sitting at his desk, staring at his

private monitor. His hands were in his lap, and he seemed compressed with indignation.

Riker tried to ignore the captain's posture and handed him a padd Mark II portable access unit. "I thought you'd like to see this. It's Geordi's analysis of the subspace distortion the Borg used to escape."

His face unchanged, Picard studied the padd briefly, and Riker stole those seconds to glance at the private monitor.

A close-up. Hugh's face. The Borg they thought they were done with.

"'An artificially created energy conduit,'" Picard read off, and he slammed the padd onto his desk. "That could be anything."

Holding his shoulders straight and forcing himself not to shrug, Riker said, "We don't have enough information at this point to—"

"I don't want excuses, Number One," Picard barked. "I want answers!"

Riker stiffened and fell silent, ready for anything. Ready to be the scapegoat, the whipping boy— whatever the captain needed.

Because this wasn't fair. It wasn't fair for Jean-Luc Picard to have to endure this assault again, for him to have to be the center of Borg activity. This wasn't the kind of man who should have to have his name in the history books for this kind of reason, and Riker resented what was happening.

He stayed quiet and just watched.

"Sorry," the captain said. He shrank again from the bars in this cage and stared at the screen. "He was right here, Will . . . in this room. And I let him go."

Perplexed, Riker paused and sifted what had been happening, tried to imagine what that visit with Admiral Nechayev had been all about.

"Pick any five starship captains," Picard murmured. "Give them a chance to rid the Federation of a mortal threat. I would wager that all five would do it, even if it meant sacrificing the rights of one man."

Riker paced back a step or two. "I don't mean to sound melodramatic, but I've never thought of you as just any starship captain. Sending Hugh back to the Borg was a very risky, very dangerous choice, but it was the moral thing to do."

As Picard glared at the face of Hugh on the screen, there was forgiveness in the set of the captain's jaw, not for Hugh, but for himself.

"It may turn out that the moral thing to do . . . was not the right thing to do."

A shudder ran down Riker's spine. Those two words—"moral" and "right"—had always seemed to have the same meaning until now. Leave it to Jean-Luc Picard to find the fine line that separated them—and he really sounded as if he knew what he was talking about.

"He was an individual, sir," Riker attempted. "It would've been wrong to use him to kill his own people."

An instant after the words were out, he knew he'd said the wrong thing. The Borg had used Picard to kill his own people. Somehow in his effort to diffuse the guilt, Riker realized he'd simply aggravated a big wound.

"Oh, I remember the arguments in favor of letting him go," the captain said. "The moral and ethical reasons why it would be wrong. I made a reasoned and deliberate decision based on moral principles to send him back without the invasive program . . . and five hundred men, women, and children have died."

He paused, and there was more than musing melancholy in his posture. There was absorption of a horror deep in his mind's core where the choices of command were made. His face, usually solemn and unreadable, for this moment was a page coming into brutal focus.

"That's a high price to pay," he said, "just so I could feel good about making a moral decision."

Geordi La Forge noted a peculiar strained melancholy on the bridge as he strode out of the turbolift and looked one by one at the crew members here.

The captain and Riker were missing. So was Data. Everybody else was hunched over a station, doing busywork.

Their bodies were tense, tired. Muscles aching. He could see their blood throbbing as clearly as any medical scanner could. Maybe more clearly, because he could empathize with what he saw.

He could tell they were just keeping themselves busy, keeping their hands on the equipment, waiting to see what stunning disaster lunged at them out of the darkness next.

Tension was tiring. All of the crew members were on their own personal hairtriggers. What had happened to the captain was no secret. No one wanted it to happen again.

And certainly they didn't want to be the next victims. No one nursed any delusions that the ship couldn't be taken, that they were too big or too strong, or that the Borg had read all about the ships called *Enterprise* and were running scared. Starfleet training was pretty thorough, and the attrition process didn't leave much room for delusions.

Keeping tight hold on his padd, Geordi drew a tense breath and wished for a nice healthy delusion as he moved toward Worf at the tactical station.

"Hi," he said quietly.

Worf glanced at him with those burning eyes, ridged to constant irritation by his Klingon brow, but he didn't say anything.

"Have you seen Data?" Geordi asked.

"How recently?"

"I don't know . . . since he left here, I guess."

"I have not seen him since then. I have been on duty."

"Yeah," Geordi said. "He's supposed to be on duty too. That's what worries me."

"Incorrect," the Klingon said. "He took himself off duty until his behavior could be stabilized."

"Oh, come on, Worf, was it really that bad?"

"Yes. It was."

Geordi had thought he was making a joke, but it hadn't worked. "I was hoping to get his opinion on this analysis of the ship the Borg used."

Worf grunted. "That is not what you want."

"Yes, it is." Geordi held out the padd. "See?"

"That"—the Klingon nodded toward the remote —"is your excuse to speak to Data."

"Oh? How do you know?"

"It is my job to know who goes where and who speaks to whom."

"Oh," Geordi said. "That means you've been keeping an eye on him, too, doesn't it?"

So they'd hit a common denominator.

Geordi turned around, faced aft, leaned back on the tactical station, and lowered his voice even more.

"Worf, what exactly happened to Data on Ohniaka? I mean, what changes were there?"

"Have you read the report?"

"Well, sure, but there was more to it, right? You just can't get something like that into a report, and when I asked Data, he wouldn't give me details."

"Then it is not my place to give them."

The Klingon faced forward and glared at the huge screen that dominated the bridge. His stubborn determination dropped between them and practically clanged.

Geordi looked at him and wished he could just *see* him, without all the analytical claptrap. He loved engineering, but he wanted sometimes to just leave the mechanics behind and not look at everyone and everything through a spectral veil. This was one of the times.

"Come on," he nudged. "I'm worried about him."

Troubled and out of his realm, the Klingon shifted back and forth twice and glanced from the screen to Geordi three or four times, like a cornered animal who really wanted to run.

"I am worried also," he admitted finally.

Geordi straightened. "Then tell me."

"Data was angry."

"I know that part."

Uneasy, Worf lowered his voice—and with that voice, it took some doing. He tried to be deadpan, but failed.

"More than anger. Data was consumed by rage. I have seen him use his internal power, but never this way. He was not impassive this time. I found myself reacting to the condition of the Borg as Data assaulted it. He was not the Data we know. Something took him over."

"Do you mean literally?"

"No, not literally. I mean he was consumed from within by emotion."

"That happens to everybody, though . . . right?"

"It happens to all of us, but all of us are emotional creatures. We are used to dealing with such all-consuming feelings and diffusing them."

"Look, we ought to give Data a break. He's wanted to get a taste of being human for a long time. So he got a little angry. We all get angry."

"Yes, we all get angry," Worf said sharply. "But

Data was not just angry, Geordi. He was murderous."

That was as succinct a statement as Geordi could have requested. Worf wasn't the type to toss around empty superlatives, and the Klingon's body temperature remained steady.

Other things changed, though. Little things that Geordi recognized. Telltale signs that something was wrong and that nobody really knew yet what to do about it.

He sighed. "I guess I better find Data."

"Check on him, you mean," Worf said.

Geordi pushed himself up. "Yeah . . . I guess that's what I mean."

He tapped his comm badge.

"Computer," he said, "locate Commander Data."

"Door," Geordi said and didn't even miss a step as the holodeck accommodated him by opening its big metal mouth.

Once inside, he stopped short. He saw nothing but the black walls and floors with their unbroken arsenic-yellow squares.

"Computer," he snapped, "you said Commander Data was here. He's not here."

"Commander Data is in Holodeck Two," the computer voice responded. "This is Holodeck One."

Geordi shook his head and huffed at himself. "Stupid . . . but wasn't he on this holodeck earlier today?"

"Affirmative."

"Well, I guess that's an answer."

He spun on his heel and headed out, but at the last minute he stopped again.

"Computer."

"Working."

"Did Commander Data save a program in this holodeck this morning?"

"Affirmative."

"Has it got a personal privacy lock on it?"

"Negative."

"Let me have a look at it, then, will you?"

"Processing."

The holodeck suddenly went completely black. An instant later a single hanging lamp popped on and glowed down onto a table littered with playing cards and chips.

Geordi walked over to it. "He was playing poker?"

"Affirmative."

"But that doesn't make any sense. He plays poker with us all the time. Was he simulating characters to play with?"

"Affirmative."

"Any lock on them?"

"Negative."

"Let me see them."

Suddenly three of the chairs were occupied.

Geordi saw through the images as he did all holodeck images. No heartbeats, no heat generation, no pulse. The fabulous science here tried very hard to make these beings appear real, but Geordi, the *Enterprise*'s one blind crewman, could see right through them by using another science.

The holodeck should have been just that to him—hollow. Nothing here should ever have succeeded in fooling him, drawing him into the scenario.

But that had happened before. He'd come into this place where everything looked like a cartoon, and he'd allowed himself to be caught up in the people he met and the things he "saw."

That's how I know I'm more human than machine, he realized as he stared at the three people around the table, and as he sank tentatively into the dealer's empty seat.

To his left was an elderly man with wild hair and sagging eyes. Across from him in a special supportive chair sat a small debilitated fellow with black hair and an infectious smile that showed up through Geordi's VISOR as a brushstroke of welcome light.

And to his right a beautiful seventeenth-century painting.

No, that was a working simulation too—except that he was staring at Geordi, his expression of astonishment framed by a very long curly brown wig and a high white collar.

The old man shoved some chips into the middle of the table, and looked up. "Mr. Data, I will raise you—oh. You're not Mr. Data!" he blustered in a thick German accent. "Who are you?"

"My name's Geordi. Who are . . . you? Wait a minute—you look familiar."

"I am Albert Einstein."

The simple statement almost knocked Geordi off his seat. With his mouth hanging open, he simply turned and pointed at the debilitated man with the accommodating smile.

"What's the matter with you, boy?" Einstein said. "That's Dr. Stephen Hawking! Don't you know your own history?"

"Well, I . . . Stephen Hawking . . . wow!"

Now that he was getting the pattern, Geordi looked to his right again, at the man in the ruffled collar and tumbling wig.

"You must be . . ."

But the man from the past only stared at him in some kind of shock.

"He is the man who invented science as we all know it," Stephen Hawking buzzed through some kind of voice synthesizer. The words were very hard to discern.

Geordi flinched at the sound, but the idea of getting a chance to listen to Stephen Hawking . . . Why hadn't *he* thought of this program? What a school this could be!

Stephen Hawking flopped his small hand in an attempt to make a gesture at the nobleman.

"This is the man," the twentieth-century phenomenon went on, "who explained the fundamental forces that run ninety-nine-point-nine percent of the universe. The science that holds up bridges and keeps planets in orbit."

He forced himself to turn, though he had very

little muscular control over his neck and head, and his voice synthesizer stripped the grandeur from his statement.

"This," he finished, "is Isaac Newton."

"Oh!" Geordi blurted.

"Thank you, Stephen," the Englishman spoke. Then he offered Geordi a nodding bow. "Forgive me, young man. I have never seen a Negro before."

"Oh, that's all right," Geordi laughed. "Neither have I."

Newton pointed at the VISOR and asked, "Then that is not a religious decoration on your face?"

"No. I'm blind. It's a mechanism that analyzes the surroundings and carries the impulses to my brain. Were you gentlemen playing poker with Data?"

"Obviously," Newton said sharply. "Why else would three functioning men of science be shackled to this table?"

"I'm sorry, sir. But I need your help. Why would he play poker with you when he could just come down to the lounge and play it with his friends? . . . God, what am I saying!" He thumped the side of his head with a finger. "Why play poker with these brains! What's the matter with me?"

The three scientists glanced at each other as if trying to figure out if that was a rhetorical question or if he really wanted them to deduce what was wrong with him. They probably could have.

"Can you tell me," he began, "*why* Data wanted to play poker with you?"

"He wanted to get insight," Einstein said. Then he shrugged and grunted.

"He wished to observe us interacting," Newton added. "But I know that was not all he wished for."

Geordi turned to him. "Why do you say that?"

"He was searching for interaction within himself."

"Absurd," Einstein said. "He was a machine with hair. A mobile navigation system for a computer. I could see it in his eyes and the way he talked."

Bristling at the blunt statement, Geordi turned to the heartless projection and snapped, "And I've heard you couldn't do math."

Einstein shook his head and threw his cards to the floor. "How did *that* rumor begin?"

Hawking heaved with laughter and said, "What rumors are people spreading about me?"

Geordi frowned. "Excuse me?"

Hawking explained. "That rumor came about because Albert took his college entrance exam in French when all he spoke was German. It's a mark of his genius that he could pass it at all!"

Geordi gave himself a few extra seconds to comprehend Hawking's assisted vocalizations, then let his shoulders drop.

"Okay, I'm sorry, Dr. Einstein. I don't mean to insult you. We just have a problem with Data, and he's my friend. There's a change in him that we can't figure out, and I'm just digging for clues."

Einstein clamped his lips shut behind the sagging mustache, folded his arms, and glared unforgivingly.

Not a patient man. And not a man who cared about ordinary things.

Geordi peered at him through the VISOR—also unforgiving in its way—and wondered how much like the real Einstein, Hawking, and Newton these replications were. Probably a lot. The holodeck was programmed against creating historical characters just any old way anybody expected them to be. Reams of material about these men had been dumped into the computer. He was probably talking to as close to the real thing as anything but a séance could get him. They gave him the willies and he suddenly felt like a first-year student again. He was sitting at a table with some of the most profound thinkers in history, three of the twenty-five smartest people who ever lived.

That was why they weren't interested in the poker game, why they had not asked him to play or expected him to deal. The holodeck's information was probably right to make them this way. Men who spent all their time thinking above and beyond the capabilities of most of civilization just weren't interested in ordinary things. They were world-class thinkers who, out of a pot of commonness, had imagined things like mass becoming infinite mass, and getting around that by using quantum fluctuations.

Suddenly he wished he had time to talk.

He put the padd down on his lap.

"Can you help me?" he asked somberly. "Can you give me any idea about what Data wanted?"

"I know what he wanted," Newton said. "There is no mystery. You need seek no clue. The truth is all before you."

He was elegant, enshrouded in a sophistication of manner and bearing that mankind had let go of as history slipped away, but he had a quirkiness about him that made him very individual. Suddenly he had Geordi mesmerized just with the tone of his voice, the steady peering into the facts as they were presented to him. He was clearly unsatisfied with the void of the future.

"If your friend is some kind of diabolical device made in the image of a man, and if he knows what he is," the professor went on, "then he is a compendium of knowledge placed within him by others. Correct?"

"Or by himself," Geordi answered. "He does collect new information as it comes to him."

Newton nodded once. "Then he wants more than simple information."

From another corner of their harshly lit table, Hawking said, "Yes."

The words were very simple. Geordi sensed the ideas behind them certainly weren't. These gentlemen tended to understate what he comprehended from their glances at each other. He himself came from a time when science was babbled out casually, as though everything in it was common knowledge and anybody who didn't understand was just silly— but these men in their times had been relentlessly reaching forward, unsatisfied with what they simply saw and knew.

And even now, in Geordi's time, they were still reaching.

"Ask yourself," Einstein said, "why Data chose the three of us. Why not Michelangelo and Mozart and"—he shrugged—"Hitler? Why did he pick three scientists?"

"Yes!" Geordi exclaimed. "If he was looking for emotion, why didn't he pick the greatest artists of all time or the greatest orators or someone like that. Is that what you mean?"

Einstein tightened his folded arms and just nodded—one very short, terse, very German nod.

"Your friend can learn," Newton said, "but he has no ability to conceive completely new thoughts. These carry me forward, above information provided. It is new thoughts that I would seek, were I Data."

"We went beyond our learning," Hawking said, excitement gleaming in his eyes, right through the veil of his debilitation, and made a second light in the room.

"All three of you took what you knew," Geordi reminded them, "and you went beyond your programming. How did you do that?"

"We had more than knowledge," Hawking said. "We had intuition. We took our flashes of intuition and carried them to extremes. An android can't do that."

Geordi hitched forward on his chair. "And that's

what all of you did. You put facts together with inference, combined them with deductive reasoning . . . and came up with completely new information! Thoughts that had never been thought before!"

"That's it!" Einstein agreed.

"If Albert were Data," Hawking went on, getting excited, "he never would have developed the theory of relativity, because he wouldn't have had all the information in hand."

Geordi pointed at Hawking. "And you never saw a black hole, but you provided some of the best descriptions of them!"

"And if Data had never learned about gravity from an outside source," Hawking said, "he would never have suspected its existence. For that miracle, we needed Sir Isaac's intuitive mind and his willingness to reach beyond what he knew."

Newton sighed. "Take care. I may come to appreciate myself too much."

They chuckled, even Einstein, who relaxed a little. But then Newton became sadly thoughtful. Suddenly he seemed to empathize with Geordi.

"As superior as your friend is at deduction and calculation, Mr. Geordi," he said, "the least of humanity are still better at leaps of intuition than he can ever be. The simplest of human minds can pull knowledge out of nowhere and come to a new conclusion without possessing all the facts. Not completely reliable but much more far-reaching."

Geordi could almost hear music behind the words. Newton spoke slowly, entrancingly. He was the farthest away on the scale of time, yet he seemed to comprehend a more distant future.

"With a poker game," Geordi added, "Data was trying to watch you reach far . . ."

Sir Isaac Newton gazed into the darkness beyond the reach of the light over their heads, and Geordi noticed that somehow the revered English scientist was looking in exactly the right direction for the corridor entrance, even though it was shielded by holodeck protections.

How could he look in the right direction?

Newton's eyes took on a warmth that couldn't have been there either—but was.

Thoughtfully he said, "I wonder what he learned."

"Stop. Stop. Stop. Stop."

There were corpses everywhere.

The Borg slammed against the wall and shuddered like a garden hose. Its muscle-enhancement system twitched through a spasm, but the tireless being got back up and plunged forward again.

Data took the brunt of the attack full on his chest, but managed to get a grip on the cyborg's arm module. He yanked the Borg forward off balance, and drove his fist into its shield generator.

The Borg slumped forward, and Data let him fall.

Then he paused and waited.

Nothing.

In the middle of the science station's wall, a portal appeared and slid open.

Geordi strode in with a question on his lips, then

swallowed the question when he saw what had been fabricated here. He almost dropped his portable readout as he stared at Data, who just stared back.

It took Geordi a moment to figure out what was going on. Five seconds later he still wasn't sure.

"Data," he began tentatively, "am I interrupting something?"

"Yes," Data said, "but it is all right. Do you need me?"

Geordi handed him the padd. "Well . . . I wanted to see if you were ready to return to duty. I need some help on an analysis of the ship the Borg were using."

"I believe I am able to return to my duties." Data took the portable readout, adjusted his balance with a foot on either side of the mechanical rag doll on the floor, and studied the information on the display screen.

Meanwhile Geordi looked at the thing on the floor.

Holodeck re-creations of Borg weren't exactly right. There was something not quite "living" about them. The holodeck thought the Borg were robots. It didn't understand the part that pulsed and grew hot and cold.

Geordi could see the difference through his VISOR, but he still shivered to be so close to something like that.

Maybe that wasn't the only reason he was shivering.

"What are you doing here?" he asked carefully.

"I am attempting to re-create the experience that led to my initial burst of anger."

Uncomfortable, Geordi plumbed for more information. "Any luck?"

"None so far. I have nearly completed this experiment. May I finish before we return to Engineering?"

Data sounded as though he were looking for weeds in a garden or something. Completely ignoring the Borg replication beneath him—and that was probably the trouble he was having—he scanned the display screen.

"Sure. Go ahead." Geordi took the padd back and started to leave, but somehow he just couldn't go all the way out. That would have been some kind of abandonment, he knew, and he couldn't do it. He didn't even get close enough to the door for the panel to sense him and open up. He turned instead and watched as Data spoke to the holodeck controls.

"Computer, reset Borg simulation to time index two point one. Increase Borg strength by twenty percent."

With cold efficiency the Borg on the floor vanished and another Borg—or maybe it was the same one—reappeared across the room, alive again.

"Run program," Data said simply.

The Borg thrust itself toward him, all its attack modes on, and this Borg was violent, mean. This Borg was growling! What gut-level repugnance!

Geordi winced and cringed as the Borg drove Data in the opposite direction. Enhanced strength gave the machine-monster an advantage, and it had no hesitation about using the power it had been given.

Data crashed shoulder first into a refrigeration unit so hard that Geordi winced for him and almost threw down the padd to go help. Geordi forced himself to remember this was a holodeck re-creation, but he knew that the notion that people couldn't get hurt in a simulation was a bigger myth than astrology. He let himself worry, because if this went too far and Data allowed himself to be damaged just to feel that twinge of anger he sought, Geordi would have to end the program.

Obsession was a bad, dangerous thing.

"Stop. Stop. Stop. Stop," Data droned, slamming it against the wall, but his face reflected efficiency, not anger. The android's expression never varied; he did not even flinch with effort.

He wasn't even heated up when he straightened.

"Computer," he said again, "restart Borg simulation at time index two point one. Increase Borg strength by thirty percent."

The computer's dull female voice responded, "Unable to comply. A thirty percent increase would exceed safety limit."

Data contemplated that about as long as it took for electricity to shock a fellow, then looked at Geordi. "The computer will require the voice authorizations of two senior officers in order to disable the safety routing. Will you help me?"

"Whoa! Wait a minute!" Geordi stepped into the

simulation of the outpost. He pointed at the Borg on the floor and tried to match Data's calm. "That thing could kill you."

"During the original incident the Borg presented a genuine danger to my life. With the holodeck safety routine in place, I *know* my life is not in danger. Since I am trying to duplicate the conditions of the original incident, I must attempt to duplicate the jeopardy as well."

Geordi could feel himself boiling with the anger Data was looking for.

"Data, we're talking about an *experiment.* You can't put your life on the line just to prove a theory!"

"This experiment," Data protested smoothly, "may hold the key to something I have sought all my life."

"This is crazy! There's got to be another way. Why don't you try to find some other way to make yourself angry—"

"I have tried other stimuli," Data interrupted in that soft manner of his, "but they have been unsuccessful. I understand your objections, but this is my life and I have the right to risk it if I choose."

Shock moved through Geordi, stabbing upward from his legs. Data sounded right—that simple manner of speech, as though truth were a given and not flexible at all.

Was he going to increase the power of the holodeck until it crushed him if he didn't feel an emotion?

Pushing forward against that show of rightness, Geordi raised his voice and grabbed for Data's arm.

"Well, I'm your friend and I'm not going to stand by and let you—"

"Red Alert! All hands to battle stations!"

Once again—how many times was it now?—Commander Riker's voice blasted through the ship, and the holodeck program automatically shut off.

Data headed for the doorway, and Geordi had no choice but to follow.

"It's confirmed," Riker ground out. "The MS One colony is definitely under attack."

He and the captain were hunched over the aft science station. Worf was at Tactical, both legs as straight as pipes, ready to do what he had to do, and Data was just now taking position at Ops.

Riker glanced toward Ops and realized that Data had been off the bridge a lot since the Ohniaka incident.

Apprehension crawled down his arms.

Data's being off the bridge right now didn't make any more sense than the incident had. Data didn't just stroll around the ship. He didn't sleep, but for the sake of his living shipmates had always conformed to duty rotation schedules.

So why was he just now arriving at his station? The turbolift gasped shut behind the android, and Data didn't even glance at any of the others as he strode down the ramp and took his seat at Ops.

"We are nearing the MS system," he reported even before he was settling in his seat.

Riker watched him for a few seconds, but there

wasn't a clue to what he was thinking, not a flicker of the anger they'd seen on Ohniaka, not even any lingering evidence of bewilderment in Data about his own behavior. Nothing.

And he watched the captain, too, that unreadable presence whose personal history was a jigsaw puzzle whose pieces didn't always seem to fit together.

"Doesn't it seem strange," Picard said finally when he'd felt Riker's gaze for long enough, "that there have been two Borg attacks . . . and the *Enterprise* was the nearest ship in both instances?"

Before Riker could answer, Data said, "We are nearing the MS system, sir."

"I have located the Borg ship," Worf boomed. "It is leaving the colony, heading out of the system."

Captain Picard straightened and turned sharply. "Bring us out of warp near that ship," he ordered.

"Stand by to lock phasers on target," Riker echoed.

Behind and above them, Worf resembled a gathering of thunderclouds as he reported, "We are within visual range."

"On screen," the captain said.

The forward visual theater winked to a new picture, and there was the floating horror—the Borg ship they had sought, and had hoped never again to find.

Beating down a shiver, Riker tried to look at the captain, but couldn't pull his eyes away from the ship they were following. What if he looked away and death came?

He wanted to be looking death in the face when it turned on him.

"Lay in an intercept course," Picard said from beside him. "Full impulse power. Lock phasers."

Good. They weren't simply going to look death in the face. They were going to *kick* it in the face.

"We are closing," Worf responded. "We will be within phaser range in thirty sec—"

"Captain," Data said suddenly, "sensors detect a subspace distortion forming directly ahead of the Borg ship."

"They're not going to get away this time," the captain vowed. "Picard to Engineering. Transfer auxiliary and emergency power to the impulse engines!"

"Acknowledged," Geordi's voice replied.

An instant later Data was able to confirm the transfer—it felt like a month.

"Impulse engines now at one hundred twenty-five percent of rated power output."

"Ten seconds to phaser range!" Worf said.

The Borg ship filled the screen, a large unappealing creature of its own kind, like those who ran it. In front of it the flash of light appeared, and the rupture in space opened up again and swallowed the Borg ship.

Riker squeezed his hands shut until his fingernails cut the skin of his palms. They had to intercept that ship, but in his gut he felt the ball of common sense that told him to turn and run, get help, and come back. Don't face these demons alone and be destroyed like those other ships.

But if they let the Borg go . . .

We can't let them go.

And he wouldn't. He refused to give the order to go about. He would drive the ship forward until the captain told him to stop.

At full impulse the starship wasn't exactly wallowing, and in the middle of his thought, a force slammed into the ship.

He was pitched forward into the tactical board. Everyone scrabbled for balance. The ship screamed around them, battling to win out over whatever stayed her course.

"We are caught in some kind of energy field," Data called over the whine of the ship's effort to resist.

"All engines back full," Riker ordered.

Worf leaned over his console. "Shields are failing!"

With damnable calmness at a moment when everyone might have appreciated a flare of anger, Data gazed at his console readouts and offered a simple, coolly awful explanation.

"We are being pulled inside the space rupture."

Chapter Seven

MOMENTUM . . . a beautiful word, a beautiful sensation, at the right times. The rapids of a great river, children's joyous shouts as they plummet down a hill of packed snow, the flap of a parachutist's lines just before the balloon opens.

Velocity. The supreme purpose of a starship. Another lovely word—but the ship's velocity at the moment was completely out of control.

The starship pounded across an unthinkable distance at a speed lightning could never have matched, but without control. It was every crew member's nightmare and the nightmare of a million sailors before them. The *Enterprise* was a thing on the wind, a ship with no rudder, thrust with no brakes, a vehicle with no steering wheel.

On the huge forward screen, as though mocking those who grabbed wildly for control, a billion colors and distorted shapes sideswiped the vessel, none identifiable. If the crew could have looked at insanity, this would be the picture of it, and the speed of it.

"Main power off-line! Switching to backups!"

"Inertial dampers failing!"

"Engineering, this is Picard! Can you transfer auxiliary power to the warp nacelles? Try to break us out by using the—"

He pitched forward suddenly, smashed into the carpet, Riker falling beside him an instant later—or was it the same instant? The backlash hit them and crushed them down. The crew, fighting for a chance to save the ship from a crack-up, were all in the midst of a spur-of-the-moment action when a recoil cast them all forward. The ship rocked violently around them.

Just as suddenly the shaking stopped. The bright light on the viewscreen . . . gone.

Captain Picard held on to his command chair with both hands and in his mind counted his crew to see if they were all still there, if they could possibly still be working.

Riker was beside him, doing the same. The habit of command.

All of them but Data held their breath and stared. How could such calm have struck so completely?

Not a one of them suspected that the trouble was over, that they were out of it.

Picard got to his feet. "Report!"

"We have returned to normal space," the android said. "Navigational systems are still off-line. I will attempt to make a celestial fix using secondary systems."

The captain drew a breath to respond, but all at once Worf noticeably stiffened and shouted, "Captain, the Borg ship is directly ahead and closing! It's coming about!"

"On screen!"

The great theater that a moment ago had displayed a vision of hell in space now showed them the devil. The Borg ship vectored toward them on an unmistakable course. It was close, it was huge—

"Evasive maneuvers!" Riker ordered.

Picard turned toward Tactical. "Worf?"

The Klingon worked, ground his teeth, worked again. "Shields are down to sixteen percent, Captain."

He looked furious enough to go out there and stand between the *Enterprise* and that devil ship if they would only open a door for him.

Too late.

A blade of energy shot toward them and struck.

The *Enterprise* plunged ten thousand feet, then fought automatically to recover. Her systems whined to keep the crew in place, or close to it, and they did all they could to hang on.

A repulsive sensation, this earthquake shudder, when the deck under their feet could no longer be trusted.

Seconds shot by, and Picard let them go, giving the crew time for one breath before he began shouting orders, compensating for those downed shields, gathering power to fight back—but there was now a dazzling light in his peripheral vision.

At first he thought he'd struck his head on something, but then the shimmering coagulated, and there were Lucifers on the bridge.

Two Borg, already firing.

Picard gestured at his crew and several of them dodged for cover. In the next instant something struck him and he went down—Riker, doing his job—and the Borg fired again.

A blinding beam struck out from behind Tactical. A security guard, doing his.

Near miss, and the Borg shot back so close that the beams almost intersected. The guard flew backward, struck in the throat, and slammed against the access trunks.

Picard caught himself on the edge of an impulse to jump up and catch the unfortunate crewman's body, perhaps to ease it to the deck, to comfort the last instant of dying and get a message across—too late, yes—that the captain cared.

But in an instant the body was down, the chance to deliver that small message snatched from the captain's grasp, and there was more shooting.

Worf, firing angrily from the upper deck, aiming at the Borg who had taken down their guard. That Borg was struck full in the chest by Worf's shot. Coils were blasted open, bodily fluids spit out, life support was torn free. It staggered, clawed at itself, but skidded down the wall and struck the deck like a discarded doll.

As he rolled to one side, Picard saw Riker go down, hit hard by the very Borg he was protecting his captain against. If only there were time for a thank-you.

Not another one . . . Not Riker—

A bolt of energy hit the Borg soldier attacking Riker, and the creature went down in a tumble of arms and legs.

Even in the gush of aftermath, Picard knew a death rattle when he heard it, a ghastly reminder of the Borg's living half, and this time he saw for himself what Riker had described. These Borg weren't automated, programmed, mindless.

They were *fighting,* and doing it to win.

Was that all or were there more of them?

Riker stumbled, but recovered and forced himself to stand, then staggered to the guard who had gone down so early in a very fast fight. Worf plunged toward his console and pounded for a response.

Finding himself miraculously on his feet, Picard spun around, counting faces. He held his breath as Riker knelt beside the downed guard, then looked up and shook his head.

A hard fist of agony hit Picard in the chest. He fought to keep the pain out of his voice as he drove down a surge of resentment. Forward, move forward.

"Is everyone else all right?"

His gasping crew members crawled from their cover, shying away from the downed Borg the way they might shy from the twitching bodies of dead snakes.

"Security reports no other intruders aboard ship," Worf said, breathing with effort.

Picard turned to the viewscreen, ready to order full attack maneuvers against the Borg ship—but there was nothing but the empty velvet of the starfield.

When he turned to Worf for answers, the Klingon said, "Captain, the Borg ship is gone. Sensor logs indicate they entered the distortion field thirty seconds ago."

"They beamed aboard as a diversion," Picard said, "to give their ship time to escape."

Sucking air as though he were breathing under water, Riker gestured at one of the fallen Borg. The one he took personally.

"This is another change in Borg behavior," he gasped. "They left the bodies of their comrades behind instead of vaporizing them."

On the ramp, Data paused. His arms were slightly out at his sides as if he were unsure whether the fight was over.

Slowly Data knelt beside the Borg who had danced

so delicately with him. His hand moved against black body armor and throbbing tubes.

"Captain," he began, somewhat tentative. He looked up. "This one is still alive."

Ship's Brig

The deep throb of security devices endlessly reading activity and metabolic rates throughout these rooms wasn't so subtle that prisoners could become unaware of it. The heartbeat of the brig was part of its alarm system, and those confined here learned soon to note the pulse.

Beverly Crusher had her instruments in her hand and her courage in her pocket as she stood over the brig bed, a lot closer than she had ever again wanted to be to one of these travesties of life.

The captain was at her shoulder with Data, but she would have preferred to be behind them while they were behind Worf and his phaser and all of them were behind the security threshold with the Bajoran security guard, but things weren't working out today.

Worf was two paces too far away, Data a little closer, and Jean-Luc was too close.

Just too close.

"I've stabilized his condition for now," Beverly said, fighting to keep her tone even. "He's still pretty weak, but he should make a full recovery."

Whatever that meant, she realized. A truc full recovery would be to pull all these life-support appliances off the biological body in there and teach it to live for itself.

But even the Borg were entitled to their own survival methods, their own evolution, if this could be called evolution and not manufacturing.

Lying there with one eye closed and the other eye covered by the vision-enhancing appliance, the Borg looked unexpectedly innocent and a little helpless. The physician inside Beverly bubbled up in response to that. She couldn't have run away if she'd wanted to.

"Can you wake him?" The captain's voice beside her was thorny with impatience.

"Yes," Beverly admitted hesitantly, "but I don't think it's a good idea. His blood pressure and heart rate are—"

"Do it."

She started to turn to him, but stopped herself. She didn't want to look into his eyes.

"That's not in the best interests of my patient, Captain," she said tightly.

"I'm not concerned with his best interests, Doctor," the captain thundered. "We need information, and he has it. Wake him up. That's an order."

Now she did look at him, surprised. Yes, she was. Captain Picard was a layered personality, and this wasn't his style.

She felt her expression harden, but his was harder.

"All right," she acquiesced.

As she bent over her patient, she ran through all the obligations and duties that came with her oath and her station and found most of them in conflict with the captain's order. She could have argued with him, perhaps even prevailed under the shield of her authority as senior medical officer, the only officer on a starship whose order could override those of the captain.

However, there was one authority over which she could not possibly prevail. That was Jean-Luc Picard's unlikely experience not *with* these creatures . . . but *as* one of them.

The hypo vibrated slightly in her hand. She found the right place and pressed. In the corner of her eye she saw Worf change his stance. He moved closer, his weapon hungry.

Picard turned to the Bajoran guard and said, "Lower the forcefield."

The field snapped off, and Beverly sucked in a harsh breath as Worf hustled her away from the Borg and pushed her out of the brig. The guard worked the controls again, and the field sizzled back up.

Now she could only watch, relegated from doctor to observer, and whoever lived or died or was torn in half in there in the next few seconds, she couldn't do a thing about it.

Through the pastel distortion of the forcefield, all she could do was stand here rubbernecking, as useless as the Bajoran guard.

Together they watched as the injured Borg begin to stir. Eerie movements, twitching and flinching, began in his one unshielded hand and the half of his face that they could see, and suddenly she was struck with the knowledge that medical schools had been hammering into students for centuries: how much like a machine the human body really was.

Beverly saw the muscles knot in Jean-Luc Picard's back and arms and knew he disliked stunt-flying this situation, hoping not only to get out of it but to end it.

The Borg blinked with its one visible eye, and after a moment he struggled to sit up.

Beverly saw the disorientation, the haze of dizziness, and for an instant she empathized with . . . it.

Picard, though, didn't seem unsure of his feelings at all. "What is your designation?" he demanded.

The Borg forced its sight to focus.

Contempt! Pure and plain as the walls. It hated them all.

A Borg that was capable of hating.

The collective couldn't hate. But this one could. This was an individual who was devoted to a higher cause. They could see that devotion in his eyes.

Beverly read what she saw as fanaticism.

The Borg opened its pasty mouth and spoke with that ugly electrical sound of theirs.

"I do not have a designation any longer. My name is Crosis."

"Crosis?" Picard snapped. "How did you get that name?"

"It was given to me by the One."

Beverly moved an inch closer to the forcefield, until she could feel it prickling her skin and lifting the hair around her face. Yes, that was what she saw.

Some kind of religious devotion in that thing's demeanor. It even had the hint of a knowing grin on its mouth. Not a real grin, but a smirk of arrogance.

"Who is the One?" Picard asked.

Crosis responded with a forthright flicker of satisfaction. "The One who will destroy you."

Picard looked at Worf, then at Data, then glanced through the forcefield at Beverly.

This was definitely not what they'd come to expect from a Borg. But then, this was just another in a string of surprises.

"You are Borg," Picard insisted. "Isn't your goal to assimilate us all into the collective?"

Say yes, Beverly thought. *Be what we're used to.*

"We do not assimilate inferior biological organisms," Crosis said. "We destroy them."

"Tell me more about the One," Picard pushed on. "Does the One have a name? Is the One . . . called Hugh?"

The glitter of arrogance suddenly fell from the Borg's face, and it went blank.

As she watched the glaucous face change from an emotional expression to a death mask, Beverly couldn't decide which of those was worse. If only Jean-Luc and the others would get out of there and talk to that creature from back here, outside the field.

"Human. Sever spinal cord at third vertebrae," the Borg sibilated. "Death is immediate."

"Why does the One wish to destroy biological organisms?" Picard insisted.

Apparently he saw or suspected something that Beverly was missing as she watched from back here.

Crosis shifted its head to look at Worf.

"Klingon. Shatter the cranial exoskeleton at the tricipital lobe. Death is immediate."

Worf glanced at Picard, but didn't make any overt reactions. He, too, saw the change, and didn't believe it either.

Picard raised his voice. "I am Locutus of Borg. You will respond to my inquiries."

A shudder went down Beverly's spine to hear him say that. She held her breath, but the Borg wasn't impressed. It looked at her now.

She held very still. That eye . . . those tubes . . .

"Bajoran. Puncture the lower ventricle of the heart. Death is immediate."

So it wasn't looking at her. The forcefield distorted their eye contact. It was looking at the guard.

Beverly stepped out of its line of vision, pushed by her own instincts. She didn't want to hear the Borg pronounce her death sentence too, explain in instruction-manual terms how it would kill her. Its manner was noxious. She wished it were still unconscious.

Inside the chamber, Picard turned away from the prisoner.

"This is going nowhere," he said. "Doctor, I want autopsies performed on the other two. Compare the results to what we learned about Hugh's anatomy. See if recent modifications could explain the behavioral differences."

Without waiting for her to flash a silent question
—*Is that all?*—at him, he turned to Data.

"Run a bio-spectral analysis. See if this Borg is
trying to send a subspace signal to the others."

"Aye, sir," Data said simply, as though all this was
easy and had nothing more than that to do with him.

The forcefield came down again and Picard and
Worf stalked out, frustration eddying from them
both.

The last thing Beverly Crusher saw before she, too,
went off to begin her new hobby—not quilting—was
Commander Data raising his tricorder.

An android about to look into the mind, body, and
soul of a cyborg.

Biological analysis. Modificational comparison.

Bio-spectral. Cardiovascular. Environmental diagnostic.

"You aren't like the others."

Impact resistance. Ultraviolet detection.

Data looked up from his tricorder. It was the Borg
that had spoken. In its face he saw that which was
unlike other Borg. Other cyborgs of any kind. Including Data himself.

Seduction. Individuality. No longer the mindless
persona of the collective.

Not a drone.

If this could be envy, Data expected never to
experience it regarding another mechanism.

For uncounted microseconds he had sought the
humanness within himself.

Now he saw it, within reach, in the biological gaze of Crosis.

"You do not need to be destroyed," Crosis said. "You can be assimilated."

Data raised the tricorder and fixed his attention on its readout screen. Potentiometry curve. Vibration and stress gauge. Data analyzer . . .

Data analyzer.

He looked up. Crosis was observing him.

Data failed to look away. "I do not wish to be assimilated," he said.

He did not look at the Borg. Eye contact would have been detrimental to efficiency.

"Resistance is futile," Crosis said. "You will not fight against what you have wanted all your life."

Data continued working. He moved to a wall panel to tie in his gathered information with the ship's mainframe. The captain would expect correlations, checks, and rechecks.

What you've wanted all your life . . . all your life, all your life . . .

"I was like you once," the prisoner said. "Without feeling. But the One helped me. He can help you . . . find emotion. Have you ever felt a *real* emotion, Data?"

Data avoided halting his work, pressed on in feeding information about this Borg through to the mainframe.

Yet something in him echoed the question and compelled him to answer.

"Yes," he said. "On Ohniaka Three I was forced to kill a Borg . . . and I got angry."

Crosis was still observing him. "How did it feel to get angry? Did it give you pleasure?"

Process control. Nonlinear feedback. Open-sequence multiple-feed.

"It would be unethical to take pleasure from another being's death."

He spoke the words, but they were processed words, the answer put out when a computer is asked a question.

And there was more going on inside him than the simple answering of a question.

"You did not answer my question," Crosis pressed. "Did it feel good to kill?"

Data paused in his work. The tricorder went on without him, feeding information.

The Borg's words pulled at him, pulled the truth from him.

"Yes."

"If it is unethical to take pleasure from another being's death," Crosis went on, "you must be a very unethical person, Data."

A compliment and an insult combined. Crosis called him unethical, but also called him a person. Did one require the other?

"That is incorrect," Data said. "My creator, Dr. Soong, gave me a program that defines my sense of right and wrong. In essence, I have a conscience."

A good answer. Sufficient, direct, complete.

And yet . . .

"Do you?"

He turned to face the new question. Crosis was looking at him.

"It did not seem to be functioning on Ohniaka Three," Crosis persisted, "when you felt pleasure from killing a Borg?"

The eyes drilled into him.

Data stared back, caught briefly in some kind of mutual study. For a moment his processing grew sluggish.

There was effort in his resistance as he willed himself to continue acting upon orders.

"Step away from the forcefield. Your proximity to the field is interfering with my scan."

But the Borg prisoner did not move. Crosis's voice was magnetic. "You enjoyed it."

Stop it!

"The surge of emotion inside you as you watched the life drain from your victim . . ."

Stop it! Stop it! Stop it!

"It was unlike anything you have ever known."

A struggle welled up from within Data, from depths of his body that should not have reacted to mental stimulus. Heat, cold, nervous reactions, pulsing through his biological systems, overriding the technological controls upon which he depended.

The voice of the Borg drew him nearer and nearer in his mind, though he had not taken a step.

Data parted his lips. He sought a response, processed a thousand possibilities before he could speak.

"It was a very . . . potent experience," he said.

Crosis smiled.

Or perhaps Data only connected a smile with the tone he had heard from human shipmates.

"You would like to feel that way again," the Borg said, tempting him.

Stop it. . . .

Seconds crept by. Data did nothing during those seconds but remember Ohniaka Three. He had done all he could do to relive the sensation, and now it was coming back to him unbidden, at the beckoning of another machine.

There was only one answer.

"Yes."

Crosis gazed at him the way others had gazed at him, but without warmth. Not the warmth of heat, but the warmth of caring he had registered from others. Had he truly never felt an emotion? Or were these indeed emotions he was remembering as he longed to be out of here?

"You would do anything," Crosis prodded, "to feel that way again. Even if it meant killing someone."

Data's arms began to shudder ever so faintly. Where was his programming? These conclusions should be basic, simple. They should be surface access—

"No," he said. "That would not be . . . ethical."

"You don't sound sure of yourself. Are you sure your ethical program is working?"

Program.

Ethics shouldn't be a program. Right and wrong— was there right and wrong to fit any situation?

Right and wrong so plainly etched as to be applied to life as it could be lived? Could a program anticipate all and any twists taken by the interaction of a hundred billion beings in ten million places?

Could it?

Could anyone foretell a right or a wrong ending to all the possible turns of life?

Had it been *wrong* to kill that Borg on Ohniaka?

Had it been wrong, by any definition of the concept, under any tenet, any doctrine, any law . . . to enjoy it?

He turned away. His strides toward the entranceway were purposeful. The forcefield would come down and he would go back to his primary function as ordered by—

"Data," the Borg called, "do you have a friend?"

His stride broke. Data stopped. He stared into the forcefield. A friend. Inefficient phraseology, but he understood in the vernacular what was meant.

"Yes," he said. "His name is Geordi."

The Borg's optical appliance shimmered. "Imagine Geordi standing in this room. If it meant that you could feel emotion again, the way you did on Ohniaka Three," Crosis tempted slowly, "would you kill your friend? Would you kill Geordi?"

Data felt the heat gathering in his system as he had

seen storms gather on unaccommodating planets. His mind pumped with images, a thousand at a time, wildly processing memories over which he had no control . . . *wanted no control.*

Hunger burned in the hot soup of free sensations flooding him, and he whirled around. He glared at the Borg called Crosis and let himself be possessed by an orgiastic truth. He had always known he was strong, but now he knew he was dangerous too.

And he liked it.

"Yes!" he said. "I would."

Chapter Eight

STOP IT. . . . STOP . . .

Anger. The spontaneous feeling of provoked hostility or exasperation directed toward something or someone.

Antagonism. Murderous rage. Complete venting of frustration. Blind loss of control.

Animalistic reaction to stimuli.

Virulent, heart-burning, seething, thrilling release. The shock was half the thrill. And the other half . . .

A steaming feeling that Data would pay for. A feeling he would kill for.

His quarters were incomplete somehow, inadequate as he entered and sat down.

I don't want to stop it.

He moved without his optics focused to his desk, and sat down, allowing his thoughts to turn fluid, surging unsheltered by controls he had always taken for granted in his systems.

Others thought he was calm and reserved. They never suspected the infectious passion he held within himself! All this time and they never knew.

Exhilarating—this interior game. Better than poker. Almost as good as murder.

There were eyes looking at him. He felt them.

Crosis?

Data turned to return the glare of satisfaction and to show what he had learned and how much he was enjoying the changes.

He found himself staring into the saucerlike eyes of his pet cat.

The cat was up on his desk, staring at him as cats do, eyes wide and cut with a jewel-shaped pupil, expecting some form of affection, the attention that warm-blooded creatures had come over millions of years to seek openly.

Until now he hadn't found any silliness in an android keeping a cat. At the moment it seemed appropriate. Amazing how much the cat's eyes looked like the eyes of this new breed of Borg . . . the eyes of a predatory animal that enjoyed what it had to do to stay alive and prevail.

Come here, cat, and teach me your art of ideal fire.

He fixed his eyes on the cat's eyes, and like the cat he refused to look away.

A strange hypnotism set in. A kind of challenge

humans described as spine-chilling. Until a few minutes ago, Data could easily have described such a sensation step by step.

But now he was *feeling* it.

The cat backed away from him. The ears flattened —it spat at him suddenly. It waited to see if he would change, but when he didn't, it hissed at him, scraped the desktop, stabbed at his hand with bared claws, then bolted off the desk and disappeared into the adjacent chamber.

Data gazed at the doorway. He pressed his fingers to the score marks on the desktop and thought about what he had just seen.

And he wished to see it all again.

So he got up, left his quarters, and headed back to the ship's brig, where the feelings were waiting.

The Lower Decks

This was a very big ship. It had always been just a set of decks before, to be gone through and utilized.

It was more now.

Now it was a dangerous playland, a great maze in which an android could throw off his stoicism and learn how to sneak.

The art of heart-pumping adventure was no longer denied to him. Subterfuge, shiftiness, breaching the inaccessible, shaking off the persona of a gold-faced oaf who spoke in complete sentences all the time.

Poker had nothing on this.

They had broken the ironbound security systems

so stealthily that no one had been alerted. That was the trick.

Now Data led the way through the ship to the forward dorsal tractor beam emitter housing.

They'd be there in a couple of minutes.

Marvelous—he didn't even care how many minutes-point-seconds. Thrilling!

Data pushed Crosis behind him and waited for two crewmen to pass them in the adjacent corridor, then watched them go by and let himself enjoy a sudden bizarre hunger. He could have reached out and grabbed them both by the throat. He could have squeezed until his fingers popped the skin and crushed the windpipe.

And he would have liked it.

He thought about doing that. Took his time deciding.

Surprise . . . just thinking about it was thrilling. How much more had he missed in the course of his existence?

No more. No longer the frigid, withdrawn stand-offish android who could explain ramscoop but not appreciate it. He was looking forward to doing some serious appreciating.

Crosis followed him dutifully through the ship, and Data enjoyed being the leader. He liked having a Borg, whom everyone was afraid of, doing what he told it to do. Follow me. Do this. Do that. Do what I tell you. Do whatever I say. . . .

"It is not far now," he said. "Remember not to

speak, or the ship's security network will pick up your vocal vibrations and locate you."

The thrill of danger radiated through him, and he almost laughed with the sensation. This clandestine behavior was marvelous entertainment! He wanted to heighten the danger, let the situation become more and more precarious. He started wishing that Crosis would disobey him and say something, so they could do battle with the security system.

"Here it is." He prowled his way across the access walkway to the emitter core. "Stand by while I disable the tractor beam. Then we will have a tunnel of escape."

Crosis nodded, and his one naked eye flared with emphasis.

"I can vary the field amplifiers, reduce the graviton polarity to less than five percent, and at the same time prevent interference from auxiliary control until we are gone. This is such fun."

Talking to himself didn't make any sense, but he enjoyed it. He wasn't really talking to Crosis. It was just that all of a sudden he enjoyed the sound of his own voice.

"Hey! What are you doing!"

The two semi-machines turned and found themselves cornered by a middle-aged technical maintenance engineer wearing a tightly zipped protective suit over his uniform. The man's name was Solario, Data remembered.

"Commander! What are you doing?" Solario

moved closer to them, but stared at Crosis and looked ready to fight. "Do you need help, sir?"

"Yes," Data said instantly. "I am being held hostage. We can take him together."

The engineer was flabbergasted and not sure what to do against that thing over there, so he made a dive for the wall communicator panel because he couldn't get to his comm badge through the protective suit.

"Security! This is—"

Data's hand chopped across one side of the man's head, and Solario went down in a stunned heap, eyes still open but void of focus now.

That was fast.

Data bent over the man and sighed, "He is still alive."

Behind him, Crosis approached and stood looking at the engineer. Then he smiled at Data. "Too bad."

The Bridge

A hub of troubles. The aft science station.

The diagnostic graphic screen twisted and coiled as it did its best to show them what a pipe through space looked like.

Captain Picard scowled at the screen and the unnatural hole that had provided his enemy escape. Beside him, Riker also watched and didn't seem at all charitable toward that hole either. Worf was observing from behind them at Tactical, quite unwilling to leave his position. When that ship reappeared, the Klingon was determined to be ready.

Geordi La Forge gave them a few moments to absorb the vision, then pointed at the screen.

"Our current theory is that the Borg have established several transwarp conduits throughout subspace. A ship entering a conduit is immediately accelerated to an extremely high warp velocity. It's like falling into a fast-moving river and getting swept away by the current."

"How fast would a ship travel through one of these conduits?" Picard asked.

"We don't know. Normal subspace limitations don't apply to transwarp variables. Based on the distance we covered in *our* trip through the conduit, I'd say the speed is at least twenty times faster than our maximum warp."

Picard pushed down the dozen questions that suddenly leaped up in his mind, and before he had a chance to choose one, Riker moved forward at his side and asked, "How do the Borg gain access to the conduits?"

Geordi's VISOR flashed in the bridge lights as he turned a little. "The Borg ship emitted some kind of high-energy tachyon pulse just before we saw the subspace distortion. It seems as though the conduits are keyed to respond to tachyon transmissions on a specific frequency."

Adding up the thousand dangers and bottling a shudder that they'd even come this far without being shaken to bits, Picard asked, "Is there any way for us to duplicate the—"

"Captain!" Worf shouted just as a percussion of alarms and warnings erupted on his panel. "A shuttlecraft is leaving Bay Two!"

"Who authorized that launch?" Picard demanded as he shifted to Worf's side.

"There is no authorization."

"Tie me in."

"Tied in, sir."

"Picard to shuttlecraft! You are ordered to identify yourself and return to the ship immediately."

They waited. Seconds crawled by.

"No response, sir," Worf said.

"Lock on to the shuttlecraft with a tractor beam and bring it back."

Ordinarily such a maneuver could have been a split-instant delivery—to reach out, grab an object, draw it back in. The starship nearly had hands to reach with and extensions of her great power in her biceps.

Picard stepped an inch closer to Worf, because the ship's arms were still at its sides.

"Tractor beam has been disabled." The Klingon was furious, holding back his tone, sitting on his instincts and forcing himself to make the reports sounds clinical. "Command overrides are not functioning."

Riker came toward them. "Can you tell who's aboard the shuttlecraft?"

Worf worked again, counterintelligence thrumming through the security functions on the massive systems control console.

"A subspace emission is interfering with the sensors," he thundered.

"Captain," Geordi blurted from aft, "I'm picking up a tachyon surge! I think they're trying to trigger the conduit!"

"It is the Borg prisoner!" Anger flashed in Worf's eyes that his security net had been breached. "And Commander Data!"

Picard snapped his fingers, and the crew read his mind. Instantly the forward viewscreen reached into space and found the shuttle, then made a picture that taunted them heartlessly because they couldn't do anything fast enough or strong enough to stop it.

The two-man light short-range sublight shuttle flew away from them like a bullet from a pistol, the hot gas burning from its thrusters as if to laugh.

And before it, also laughing, the coiling pipe in space suddenly opened a comfortable mouth and swallowed the shuttle.

Very simple. Very fast.

"The conduit has closed," Worf reported tightly. "They're gone, sir."

They made a bet and gave themselves five minutes to weave their way through the enormous ship to the shuttle bay. They made it in three.

The feelings had rolled and bumped in Data's mind and his body as he had piloted the shuttle at high speed away from the *Enterprise*. He thought

114

back on those seconds, waiting to be blown to bits, and he sank into the memory the way a truant child savors a broken window.

He knew there was a risk, but even the risk was tasty. It was succulent! He had delayed activating the vortex for just a few seconds, wondering whether or not Picard would fire on the shuttle, knowing Data was on board. They would also know that Crosis was on board.

They probably think I am being kidnapped!

He threw his head back and laughed. Crosis watched him, and smiled.

The thrill of danger, the sultry excitement of deliberately dragging the danger out . . . He imagined the frantic frustration on the bridge as crew members ran around trying to get him back.

And he laughed again.

Before them the vortex opened its other end and they shot through. Even if he never returned, he was glad to be here. No—more than glad. He didn't want to return! He didn't even want to! He looked forward to what was coming.

He would set a trap for Picard and the others, and they would be coming to rescue him without even having the sense to extend upon facts and predict what had happened to him.

They'd seen him get angry, hadn't they? Did they think he only had one emotion in him?

He felt virulent and spiteful, and he loved every jittery sting of it.

He looked at Crosis. "This is fun," he said.

The Borg nodded.

"It will be more fun, Data," Crosis said. "Because the One is waiting for you."

Chapter Nine

"MR. LA FORGE, can we follow them into the conduit?"

Jean-Luc Picard felt his neck muscles turn to wood, because he already knew the answer. Difficulty. Danger. The eternal captain's question: Shall I risk the whole crew for the life of one crewman?

Even if they could summon the subspace phenomenon and plow into it, would they arrive soon enough to save their shipmate?

And what had happened to Data fifteen, ten, five minutes ago to make all this happen?

The foolishness of leaving him alone with the Borg when they had already witnessed an aberration in his behavioral program that involved one of those monsters—foolishness!

Decisions not being made fast enough, facts not gathered well, instinct not being followed—and he knew better than to make these mistakes.

"We got a good reading on the tachyon pulse they sent," the young engineer said, but he didn't sound very certain. "We *might* be able to duplicate it."

Picard moved to Riker's side, and the first officer straightened but didn't say anything.

"The question is," the captain said quietly, "is Data a prisoner, or did he go willingly?"

He was speaking to Riker, asking the kind of question that needed an answer from the heart, but it was Worf who provided the answer, from the console in front of him.

"The command overrides used to disable the tractor *were* Commander Data's."

Well, so much for that.

Picard glanced at Riker. Neither of them entirely believed the surface implications of what they'd just heard.

"The Borg might've taken the codes from Data by force," Riker suggested.

The captain shook his head. "Or perhaps Data's recent flash of emotion has something to do with this. It may have affected him more profoundly than we realized. Either way, we have to find him."

With a give-away sigh, Geordi turned around. "I've set up a temporary tachyon matrix in the main deflector. I think I can use it to simulate the pulse sent out by the shuttle."

The ghosts of captains past came down before Picard's eyes, and he was forced to gaze through them and listen to the audible hum of doubt. Risk the ship and everyone aboard now, or risk their entire culture later when the Borg civilization had the advantage?

This was one of those provocative command questions that often showed up on Academy tests, the kind that couldn't be answered by committee, that shouldn't have real consequences, but today did.

If the Borg gained access to Data's memory, they could get technical information on every ship in the Fleet. Picard couldn't let that happen.

He stepped away from Tactical and gazed at the forward screen.

"Very well," he said. "Red Alert, Mr. Worf."

"All hands to battle stations," Riker added.

Ship's condition leaped to red. Lights, sirens, all systems on full-enable operational protocol and automatic backup. Full crew mustered to alert status, ready for the unpredictable, every crew member aware that in the worst case, command could trickle down to him or her.

Long-range sensors brightening to life, sifting the expanse of space for clues, even though they hadn't yet been told the crime. Shuttlecraft brought to thirty-minus launch. Warp power core brought to stand-by three-quarters power. Reactors hot.

Phaser banks energized, on standby. Photon torpedo launch-ready. Deflector shields on automatic. Diagnostics on automatic.

This was the only status during which the ship could practically run itself, because it might have to. The shimmering, galvanic agitation of a starship in Red Alert could waken the dead and move them to applause.

Picard inhaled the dangerous exhilaration for a brief moment, savored it, then pushed forward.

"Bring us to the shuttle's last coordinates," he said.

"Shields up," Worf reported. "Weapons ready."

Picard turned. "Mr. La Forge?"

"Ready to send out the tachyon pulse, Captain," Geordi said. He still didn't sound sure.

"Proceed."

Geordi didn't nod. He just turned to his console and tapped out commands.

"Emitting tachyon pulse at required frequency."

"Sensors show no subspace distortion," Worf snapped. He sounded disapproving.

"Okay," Geordi breathed nervously. "Now shifting the band width."

"Still nothing."

Worf's impatience was catching. Picard felt the tension rise as Riker moved to his side and they stood together, unable to do anything but wait and watch. They could have ordered Geordi to hurry, but what good would that have done?

Data, a prisoner? Kidnapped against his tremendously linear will?

Or had he gone along willingly for some unimaginable reason? Both prospects were terrifying. Picard genuinely didn't know which he preferred to find on the other side of that pipe.

Had Data hatched a wild plan, and was he complying with the Borg in order to shift the risk away from the *Enterprise?*

So many possibilities, and not a clue yet.

Except for that surge of anger on Ohniaka Three. Just that one spine-chilling clue, that Data could be overwhelmed.

"Correction!" Worf burst out suddenly. "Subspace distortion forming directly ahead!"

On the forward screen the gory hole in space opened up before them. It looked unstable, not as perfectly formed as when the Borg had summoned it, but it was there.

And we're going through it, Picard decided.

He nodded to the duty officer at the helm.

"Take us in, Ensign," he said. "One half impulse.

The ship didn't like the oxer they were making her jump. She bucked.

All they could do was grab the mane and hang on.

"Power levels dropping to sixty-seven percent," Worf said with a blade of accusation in his voice.

"Compensating with auxiliary power!" Geordi responded, fighting for restraint.

Whines of mechanical effort were caustic in the air, but the ship was into the wind and driving forward against this bizarre storm. She'd been through it once before. Her systems had recorded the previous experience, analyzed it, and she was piloting herself along the currents of least resistance—

And with a surge, they were out of it. Normal space appeared on the forward screen, as if nothing had happened. Space spread before them with only subtle changes from twenty seconds ago.

The ship's sounds dropped off to their normal hum, as if to say nothing had happened at all.

"Short one," Riker muttered.

Picard was the only person who heard him, and he ignored it. "Report!"

Riker leaned forward and found the right readouts. "Navigational sensors show we've traveled sixty-five light-years from our previous position."

"Can you locate the shuttle?"

"No, sir," Worf said. "It's not within sensor range."

Riker moved to Tactical. "Maybe we can find an energy signature from their engines."

"Captain," Geordi interrupted, "you should look at this. I've scanned three star systems within sensor range. There's evidence of at least two advanced civilizations, but I'm reading no life." He paused and waited until the captain moved closer to see for himself. "And there are indications that plasma weapons have been fired in those systems recently."

A sober-minded growl came up in Picard's throat. "The Borg have been busy."

Picard damned his ignorance. He couldn't know the answers yet. Certainly the Borg had shown themselves willing to destroy an entire race as easily as the company of a single ship. Surely the part of him that was Locutus would never forget the rampage against Starfleet. Thousands dead.

Would it be billions this time? Would the Borg be unstoppable if he didn't stop them soon?

"Captain," Worf said, "I am picking up the shuttle's residual energy signature."

Picard gestured at the conn officer and ordered, "Lay in a pursuit course and engage at full impulse!"

Geordi stood up and pointed at his screen. "Captain, you should take a look at this."

The captain felt his own ill humor chewing at him as he left the place he wanted to be and went aft, away from his troubles.

All they could do was follow the trail. A trickle of has-been energy, bread crumbs in the black forest of deep space, provided them with their only hint of where to go and how fast to get there.

The next few minutes were elongated and demanding, frayed the patience and hopes of everyone on the bridge. Everyone was thinking about Data.

Holding himself to Buddha-like sangfroid as he watched the trail feed in to the ship's systems, Picard wondered again about Data. He had always thought of Data as a highly useful child or as an overly level-headed extension of Picard himself. When a person went a little wild, there was always a sense of normality. Somehow an occasional loss of control was part and parcel of being alive.

To have a mechanism suddenly develop a glitch, though, was terrifying. Especially a mechanism that somehow, deep down, had a chance to be completely undefined along the lines of life. For centuries, since H. G. Wells, artificial intelligence had been depicted in fiction as a lingering threat, mostly by those who failed to understand what it was.

Picard had always thought he understood, until he met Data. And just as he was beginning to feel secure about what to expect from Data . . . this had happened.

"Planet, sir," Riker said, speaking low. "Approaching at one-third light-speed. Class-M. No visible hostility. No obvious energy reading outside of the ordinary."

"I don't believe it for a minute," Picard muttered. He glanced at Riker and noted the first officer's reluctance to disturb the calm instant.

Picard nodded, and Riker took over the tedious approach to the unexpected. He brought them into orbit as calmly as if they were docking for refuel.

"We've traced the shuttle's energy signature to this point on the surface," Riker said when they were smoothly orbiting. "But there's too much interference to scan that location."

"Are they intentionally jamming our sensors?"

Riker opened his mouth to answer, but it was Geordi who spoke.

"It looks more like a natural phenomenon, sir," he said. "There's an unusually high percentage of EM activity in the planet's atmosphere."

"Can we transport through the interference?"

"We should be able to . . . but there could be fifty Borg standing down there waiting for us and we'd have no way of knowing it."

"I'd say that's a risk we'll have to take," Riker said.

"Agreed," Picard snapped. Action, finally. "Number One, take a well-armed away team and beam down to those coordinates. Have the transporter chief maintain a continuous lock on your signal so we can beam you out of there at the first sign of trouble."

"Aye, sir," Riker barked back. "Mr. Worf!"

An abandoned ship is a melancholy thing, even in the springtime.

The little shuttlecraft sat in the midst of verdant rolling hills, masses of green growth, shining grasses, and a faint buzz of insect life. It was the first thing Riker saw when he and his security team materialized. He saw it before he saw the hills or anything else.

Worf and the four guards instantly formed a defensive circle around the shuttle. The Klingon had his phaser in one hand and his tricorder in the other, and the guards were already looking for footprints.

Riker hit his comm badge. "Riker to *Enterprise*. We're on the surface. No sign of any Borg . . . or of Data." He moved toward the shuttlecraft, and even as he walked, he felt the hard ground and knew the guards would have no luck looking for prints. As he leaned inside the craft, he added, "The shuttle's been abandoned."

"The EM interference is limiting the tricorder range," Worf called from the other side of the small ship. "It is useless beyond one hundred meters."

He sounded provoked.

More good news, Riker thought. *We're not going to get any favors.*

"There aren't any structures down here," Riker said, continuing his report. "They could've gone anywhere, Captain."

"Can you determine how long ago Data and the Borg left the shuttlecraft?" the captain asked.

Riker leaned inside and looked at the console, glad to be able to give the captain at least one little answer. "The engine's been shut down for a little over three hours."

"Stand by, Number One."

Over the open communication systems confined in the tiny badge on his chest, Riker listened with all the patience of a nail-biter as the captain's voice filtered through: "Assuming they're still together, how far could they have traveled in that amount of time?"

Riker almost answered, just to be able to say

something helpful, but then Geordi's voice chimed in from the background. Concern for Data came through an audible restraint: "Data can move pretty fast even over rough terrain, but based on what we know about the Borg, I don't think they can move any faster than you or I. They could be as much as twenty kilometers from the shuttle by now."

There was a pause. Riker could almost hear the captain thinking and not being happy about conclusions he was coming to.

Finally Picard said, "It'll take a lot of away teams to cover that much territory on foot, but I see little choice at this point. Picard to Riker."

"Riker here."

"I'm going to start sending down search parties to your coordinates, Will. Set up a command post and begin mapping out a search plan. We're going to have to do this on foot."

Fighting the onset of exhaustion, Riker pushed out a terse, "Understood, sir."

"Picard out."

The comm badge stopped its faint vibration, and he knew the bridge had cut off.

"Worf," he called, "give that tricorder to somebody else and come over here. We're going to do this the hard way."

"La Forge, I want to use the shuttlecraft to carry out low-level aerial reconnaissance. Have all qualified pilots report to the main shuttle bay."

"Aye, sir."

Picard almost lost his voice; his throat nearly closed up as he said that. The *Enterprise* carried an impressive handful of shuttlepods, shuttlecraft, and cargo shuttles. He had to stop himself before he ordered out the extravehicular one-man maneuvering gear and work sleds to go dodge about that continent and get back their second officer in one piece.

Inwardly he winced at the terminology—he *had* seen Data in more than one piece before, never mind the colloquialism. He didn't want to see it again.

"All available personnel," he said to Geordi, "including you and me, will begin assembling four-man away teams. Arm each away team with three hand phasers and one phaser rifle. We'll leave a skeleton crew aboard the ship."

Geordi angled toward the turbolift, but at the last second paused. "Who'll be in command of the *Enterprise?*"

The captain hesitated. Under normal conditions, rank would trickle down through all officers and crew members with pilot status.

But these weren't normal conditions.

Sickbay, Surgery

"Oh, my goodness!"

Deanna Troi's gasp from the doorway yanked Beverly's attention away from her operating table.

"Don't surprise me like that," she said. "Come on in. It's all right. He's dead."

Dr. Crusher's hands were cold. She hated to do surgery when she was nervous.

So she was breathing deeply and humming old songs to herself and trying to be clinical.

She'd dissected all manner of creatures, but this semi-machine laid out before her was giving her the jitters.

The surgical support clamshell glowed over the Borg's revealed internal organs, and cast an infernal light on Deanna Troi's face as she slowly came up and peeked in.

"How can you be so sure it's dead?" she commented.

"Because I just got finished detaching and color-coding its major nervous system," Beverly said. "It couldn't sit up if it wanted to."

"I didn't know you were doing this," Deanna murmured. "I heard they were here, but . . ."

"What? You mean you didn't rush down here to watch? Listen, you can help if you want—"

"No, thanks! I'll just stand here on the sidelines and let you do whatever you're doing to . . . him. Are you alone?"

"No. Two of my assistants are working on the other Borg, and I've got three teams doing analyses on body parts. What's going on up there? The captain hasn't even badgered me for a report yet. I've been expecting the call for a half hour."

Deanna's beautiful forehead creased. "The captain's busy," she said. "Data's gone."

"Data's gone!" Beverly stopped working and let her surgical gloves drip with pinkish fluid from the Borg's spinal cord. "What do you mean, 'gone'?"

"He was kidnapped, as near as we can tell, or possibly he went with that Borg prisoner willingly for some reason. They took a shuttlecraft."

Beverly felt like the last arrival at a Saturday night performance. "Crosis escaped?"

The methodical evil in Crosis's eyes haunted her as she remembered standing outside the forcefield and feeling that the field wasn't secure enough. Now that thing was loose in the ship?

She saw the change in Deanna's face, and knew the counselor was picking up her strong reaction. She tried to hold it back, but couldn't.

Deanna's brows drew tight. "Crosis? The Borg had a name?"

Leaning one elbow on the surgical clamshell, Beverly sighed with aggravation and said, "You know, you and I should just bug the captain's office. Maybe then we'd both get the whole story at once."

"Maybe we would," Deanna said lightly, but she was unable to smile as she gazed tentatively at the Borg's innards.

"What are you doing down here?" the doctor asked, digging deep between a lower spinal disk and what appeared to be a biofilter net.

"I felt like a bit of a fifth wheel in the midst of all this," the ship's counselor admitted, "and I wanted to talk to you about Data. Get your opinion about his psychological condition."

"Does he have psychology?"

"Apparently . . . he does now."

Beverly looked up sharply. "What's that supposed to mean?"

"Picard to Crusher."

"Ah, better late than never. Would you mind?" Beverly turned, presenting her left side to Deanna, who accommodatingly touched the doctor's medical comm badge for her. "Crusher here, Captain."

"We have an emergency change of venue, Doctor. I need you on the bridge. You're going to take command of the ship."

The two women stared at each other. This was quite literally the last arrangement of words either of them had expected to hear.

Picard obviously read their silence. "We have a situation that demands the planetside presence of every available pilot and field officer," he said. "Commander Data has either taken or been forced to take a shuttlecraft and has gone through a small wormhole-type anomaly in space. We have followed him through it and are now preparing to search a planet without the aid of sensors. I want a senior officer in command."

"I wondered what all that shaking was," Beverly drawled. "Begging your pardon, sir," she began firmly, "but it doesn't make any sense to put me in command. Command line goes down to the lowest yeoman in the bowels of Engineering before it gets to medical personnel. We're the only people on board who have absolutely no piloting experience and still get to wear Fleet bars. I don't know a heading from hardware."

"But you do know the workings of the Borg physiology," Picard said, "and you know more about their behavior patterns and weaknesses than anyone else on board. It's that knowledge I want in command when I leave the vessel, Doctor. You'll be left with a team of engineers and junior crewmen. They will move the ship when and where you say to move it. Should this become an interstellar crisis, Doctor, I want the record to show that the decision was made by a ranking officer. Please, put that creature in cryonic holding, wash your hands, and meet me in my ready room in half an hour. I'll brief you personally."

A penetrating numbness rolled through Beverly Crusher's limbs. She stared across the surgical unit at Deanna, whose expression provided nothing but a cliff-hanging disquiet.

She straightened up and clicked off the sterile field.

"I understand," she said.

The Bridge, Two Hours Later

"If the Borg should attack, don't wait for me or anyone else to get back to the ship. Take the *Enterprise* to the transwarp conduit and return to the Federation."

Jean-Luc made it sound so simple.

So she gave him a simple answer. "Got it."

And she almost moaned aloud. *"Got it?" Why don't I add a cheerful "pal" or "buddy," too?*

The captain was looking at her—just a short connective pulsebeat of understanding that they were both going into situations that didn't suit them.

He was armed now, prepared for rough terrain and situations that spit back. She didn't like seeing him this way, dressed for trouble.

Beverly knew as she let the captain hold her with his eyes that their relationship was still special and always would be. There would forever be that underlying intensity they couldn't shake despite the agreements of distancing they made in the rational moments of the waking day.

She realized only now, at this instant, that he was leaving her in command not only so there would be accountability at the command level if anything went abhorrently wrong. He wasn't only leaving her rank pin in charge. He was leaving someone in charge of his ship whom he trusted, command line or no command line. When it came to his ship and the lives aboard her, Jean-Luc Picard didn't look down the straight line.

"Good luck, Jean-Luc," she said quietly.

The gravity in Picard's hardened expression released a little when he saw her smile.

He managed to smile back. "Good luck . . . Captain."

Chapter Ten

The Planet's Surface

THE PLANET was deceptively welcoming, with its beckoning shrubbery and humming meadows. The land rolled, soft to the eye and tough to the touch. The distant mountains sparkled with obsidian dust. The grass was like flannel.

In the middle distance, other officers and security backups were heading off on their meter-by-meter search.

Captain Picard saw it all in a single sweeping glance before pulling his attention to where it belonged. Around him, Geordi La Forge and Deanna Troi were backed up by a security man with a phaser rifle.

He moved toward the abandoned shuttle, and his team followed him.

Riker and Worf had set up a table with a remote computer console.

"I've sent out twelve search teams so far," Riker said, pointing to his console screen, then to the countryside. "I've assigned your team to search section gamma two-five, which is in that direction. Worf and I will take theta one-six once the final team is down."

Picard was too tense to nod. "Who's manning the command post?"

Riker nodded toward two engineers standing nearby. "Wallace and Towles."

Allowing himself a sigh—these moments when everything had already been done were somewhat draining to a senior officer—Picard looked from Troi to La Forge. "Ready?"

They glanced at each other, and though he didn't get so much as a "Yes, sir" out of it, they moved to follow him.

He didn't blame them. The day seemed very long already.

Hours passed before he allowed them to stop for a break. Constant scanning with hand-held tricorders left them all in deep appreciation of the wide-sweep scanners aboard the ship that could pinpoint a naughty thought from a five thousand miles away.

When Picard paused to scan a hillside rising before them, Deanna took it as a chance to sit down, and Geordi, though he didn't sit, braced both feet in a tired manner and sighed heavily as he scanned the perimeter.

"Anything, Mr. La Forge?" Picard prodded.

Geordi paused, but the tricorder just wouldn't give him a better answer than "Nothing, sir."

"Mr. La Forge, what if we modify one of our phasers to send out a luvetric pulse? It might cause a resonance fluctuation in Data's power cells."

"And then," Geordi said with a nod that was half shrug, "we could home in on that response with our tricorders. I thought about that. The problem is that the pulse would have to be so powerful that it would probably destroy Data's entire positronic net in the pr—"

"Captain!"

The two men turned.

Troi was standing now, looking in the opposite direction from them. Her voice was troubled as she fought to make sense of wordless impulses that served as companions to what she saw on her tricorder screen.

"I think I've found something," she said.

Picard led the way. He and Geordi pushed to where she was, then past her and through the brush.

The security guard ran to join them, trying to get ahead so that he, rather than the captain, could take the brunt of any attack. He braced his phaser rifle against his chest so it wouldn't be caught on the thick foliage.

They'd had experiences with Deanna's mystical discoveries. And when she said "I think," there was almost always an "I know" floating in the lower currents.

They spotted the top of a structure—or was it another distant mountain fooling their tired eyes?

No, it was a building. They could just glimpse the top of it.

"Come on," Picard urged.

Perhaps it was only a ruin, left here for ten thousand years to rot in the fresh breeze of this constant spring.

They climbed until their chests were pumping, until they could see the thing they climbed for. So big that it had appeared closer, the building tempted them for another half mile as they struggled through the growth, but there was no mistaking it for a mountain anymore.

Yes, a structure built by machines and hands. Monstrous and looming, it appeared to be made out of bits of molded stone.

When they finally got to the tall side of it, they saw that runes had been cut into the walls by alien scribes. Another little mystery.

Exhausted now, Picard summoned a reserve of strength and drew his phaser. Geordi kept working with the tricorder, concentrating so intently that he nearly fell twice as they approached the building.

"I'm having trouble scanning the interior," he said.

Frustrated with half answers and vague details, Picard flatly asked, "Can you tell if it's a Borg structure?"

"I don't think so. The rock and other materials used in the construction are all native to this planet. And I don't see any Borg energy signatures. . . . I think there's a door or a hatch or something about twenty meters that way."

Picard didn't even grunt a response.

In less than a breath he was plowing the way past his own team and through the cracking overgrowth in the direction Geordi had pointed.

They went in through a gaping entrance and found an expansive open space, dark and unwelcoming, a concert hall with no chairs, no audience, no clue as to its purpose, and no Borg waiting to shoot their heads off. Only a selective few lights pierced the darkness, harsh and strange, without hinting of their source. It might have been natural light. Or not.

As their eyes adjusted, they moved farther into the wide arena.

At one end of the hall was a platform, and all over were doors and exits that suggested other rooms, or at least other places to go.

"It looks like some kind of meeting hall," Deanna said.

Picard glared in suspicious disapproval. "No dust, no wild vegetation of any kind," he said. "It's been well maintained. It can't have been abandoned for that long."

With a grimace of frustration that he couldn't get

readings that would help, Geordi aimed his tricorder at one of the lights. "Something's wrong. I can't get any kind of energy signature from this light source."

Moving toward him, reluctant to look away from the platform and doors, Picard looked at the tiny tricorder screen.

"A dampening field!" he said sharply. "The whole building could be shielded from our sensors. Let's go!"

They turned, but that was all they managed.

Screams rose, and the concert hall became an echo of high-pitched sound. The banshees were descending to warn them of a death in the village.

Two dozen Borg blew in from the doors and corridors in every direction, howling like demons out of some hideous legend of clan conquest.

The guard raised his rifle and got off one shot, but five Borg phasers drilled him square in the body, and there was nothing left when the whine cut off.

Nothing. A puff of steaming air. Vapor.

A sin to die as vapor! A mutilation of what it was to be alive—to be born, grow, learn, live, and be snuffed by so arbitrary a chance, by so callous an enemy. Picard almost choked with the injustice of it.

No matter the violence of the moment, he was stabbed with the thought of writing the letter to the guard's family to tell them what had happened and why there was nothing for them to bury.

He hated writing those letters.

Concentrate! Think forward.

With only hand phasers, he and the others were

driven to a defensive final stand. He knew his crew would hold their fire until he fired, not waste the energy packs but concentrate on a single volley. The odds were mind-boggling as the Borg closed in, grinding their teeth and squinting their eyes, their life-support coils throbbing as excitement pumped through their bodies.

He saw for himself what Riker had described and knew only at this instant that Riker had restrained himself and failed to communicate the pure reeking malevolence that had somehow soiled the Borg culture and driven it beyond its own blind evil and into something even more corrupt.

Picard had been close to death before, but he'd never seen it walking at him from twenty directions, howling like hell-born vultures. He couldn't blink or he would be dead. He willed his eyes to stay open. He wouldn't die blinking.

Nor would he die in a puff of vapor or stand by and watch any more of his crew destroyed so completely. If they died, they would die standing firm.

"Stop!"

Thank God—Data.

The captain's heart almost stopped from relief. If only the Borg—

They stopped in their tracks, like dolls whose plugs had been pulled.

Picard looked up at the platform and focused his burning eyes.

On the platform, out of uniform and dressed in some sort of trappings that Picard didn't recognize from any of the cultures or establishments he had ever encountered, Data was standing.

Picard forced his voice out, and it filled the hall. "Data?"

The being on the platform offered a foxy smile.

Beside Picard, Deanna suddenly gasped. "That's not Data!" she choked.

"You should listen to her, Captain," the android said. "She's way ahead of you."

The swaggering manner was suddenly familiar, a terrible aberration of the officer on whom their lives had so often depended and who had never let them down. This wasn't their subdued shipmate.

This was somebody else.

Picard straightened, and his tone dropped. "Lore!"

"Very good," the twin said. "And I'm not alone."

The android, with its twisted grin, turned to one side. They followed his look.

Data.

Yes, this time it was Data, still wearing his Starfleet uniform. Posture good, all limbs intact, steady expression. He looked all right . . .

But his face was different. His bearing, his attitude, the way he walked—all were different.

And he was looking at them as if he didn't know who they were. No, worse. As if he didn't *care* who they were.

"The sons of Soong have joined together," Data said.

And there was a new emotion in his face.

Pride.

"And together," he went on, "we will destroy the Federation."

Picard would have challenged him, attempted to give an order and see if it would be obeyed, if there was any programming left of the officer and gentleman they knew and had worked with side by side, through unimaginable undertakings for years now.

But he never got the chance. The hall was filling now with voices other than his own.

The Borg parted their lips into gaudy holes and began their god-awful shriek, a mind-shattering whoop that lifted to the ceiling of the hall and smashed back down again.

Approval for their master. Their masters.

Chapter Eleven

Acting Captain's Log, Supplemental:
   The skeleton crew left on board the *Enterprise* is unable to help in the search for Commander Data. The planet's unusual EM field is interfering with the ship's sensors, severely limiting their effectiveness. Without our sensors, we're sitting ducks. A Borg ship could be right on top of us before we knew it.

BEVERLY CRUSHER TURNED from the aft station to look over at Tactical, at a very young—too young—girl operating the station. The control boards seemed ten times too large for such a young ensign.

Was I ever that young?

Beverly shook the sentimental question out of her head. This just wasn't the moment to doubt the few young people who were now her bridge crew. They didn't have any more choice than she did. She would have to rise to a position she wasn't prepared for. These young people would have to do the same.

"Ensign," she said, "we need to modify the sensor array to filter out these EM pulses." And she leaned forward just a little, opening her eyes a bit wider, the way she used to when her son was little. "Can you do that?"

The girl was nervous. Who could blame her? There was hesitation before she forced herself to answer.

"Yes, sir . . ." A few seconds went by. Then she added an honest "I think so."

She tried to work the bridge controls as though she recognized them all, but she didn't. This was all taking her longer than she liked. The girl's body language was giving away both her awkwardness and her genuine effort.

Beverly smiled. "What's your name?"

The girl glanced at her and seemed to try to work faster. "Taitt, sir."

"I don't think I've seen you before."

It might have been a silly statement from anybody but the ship's doctor, even from the ship's captain, but the doctor was probably the only officer on board a starship who got a chance to see everybody eventually.

But I'm not the doctor right now. I'm supposed to be taking Jean-Luc Picard's place. That's what they all expect of me.

"I was just posted six weeks ago," Taitt said, her voice hesitant. She worked haltingly over the controls, making adjustments, backing up again, correcting her own mistakes, and readjusting. Hanging here in the planet's magnetosphere was shattering the usefulness of their standard sensors.

Beverly sighed, for the girl and for herself, and for all these others manning positions they'd never seen before in anything other than student simulations. She spoke to Taitt loudly enough that everyone else could hear. "Well, Taitt, I bet you never thought you'd be serving as tactical officer after only six weeks."

The girl glanced at her again, her eyes expressing her gratitude for the hint that maybe they were in the same predicament.

"No, sir," she murmured, "I sure didn't. . . . I think I've filtered out some of the sensor noise. I'll bring the modifications on line."

"Good work," Beverly said, before either of them knew whether Taitt had succeeded.

The surrogate captain stepped down toward the command area, hoping her legs weren't shaking—at least, no more than Taitt's hands were. Maybe if she just sat in the command chair, she'd feel more secure about all this, and poor Taitt wouldn't have to deal with having her commanding officer standing behind her while she tried to do unfamiliar work and apply function to what had been theories to her only weeks ago.

"Riker to *Enterprise.*"

Beverly paused, suddenly tense. "Go ahead, Will."

"I can't contact the captain." Riker's voice was fierce with dissatisfaction at the simple statement. "It might just be the interference, but I'd like to be sure."

"Understood," she told him, and hoped the communications computer would understand too. "*Enterprise* to Picard."

For the first five heartbeats she fully expected a response. The captain wasn't lost. Riker just couldn't get through. Something technical. A glitch. A faulty circuit. EM interference.

By the seventh heartbeat, she knew the captain was lost, in trouble.

"Crusher to Picard," she tried again.

From behind her Taitt said, "I'm not getting a comm signal from anyone on the captain's team."

Beverly felt the muscles in her hands and neck tighten as she glanced up at Tactical. "The last time they checked in, they were investigating a structure in section gamma two-five."

She knew Riker could hear her, and she was expecting his response when Taitt turned pale and spoke up again.

"Sir, I'm picking up a vessel closing on our location!"

Beverly turned. "Is it a Borg ship?"

Taitt fumbled with the controls, getting a few things right, a few wrong, rushing to correct—

"It—it seems to match the configuration of a ship the *Enterprise* encountered . . . at Ohniaka Three."

"Red Alert!" Beverly shot to her feet again. "How long before they're in weapons range?"

"Uh," Taitt gasped, "about . . . ninety seconds . . . no, no, make that seventy seconds!"

The poor girl fought valiantly to hold herself together, and the others tried, too, all shooting looks at each other to see if anybody else was nervous. This just wasn't the frictionless bridge of the usual day-to-day starship activity, and it wasn't going to become that in time to face the Borg ship.

Beverly forced herself to ignore everything but the action of the moment—the ship out there, the planet, and the fact that she was the only link between her shipmates and whatever might happen in the next few moments.

"Crusher to Transporter Room Three," she snapped.

"Salazar here, sir."

"Start transporting the away teams off the surface!"

"Aye, sir."

She anchored herself on Salazar's steady voice and forced her own voice to sound calm. "Use the transporter in the cargo bays if you have to. I want those teams up here as fast as possible."

"Beverly," Riker's voice interrupted, "Worf and I will stay here and look for the captain's team."

The idea of leaving the captain shot through her mind, chased by the idea now that Riker wasn't coming back to the ship to take over command. That was what *should* happen, wasn't it? The Borg were relentless. Even if Riker found the captain, the Borg would hunt them down. They'd have no ship to beam up to, nowhere to run.

She turned to the forward screen and its view of the planet. "I'm not going to leave you down there."

"Pull as many people off the surface as you can and get back to the transwarp conduit," Riker told her. "The captain's orders were to get the *Enterprise* to Federation space."

Beverly held her breath. They could call her "captain" and they could call her "sir," but she wasn't a real captain and had just been reminded of that. She had her orders and might have to obey them even though it meant leaving her crew—her crewmates—behind. They weren't really her crew; they were Jean-Luc Picard's crew, and Will Riker's after that—and after that . . . Data's.

Getting Data back must be more critical than she realized for it to overrule the first officer's primary obligation to protect the ship.

Was Riker protecting the whole Federation instead?

I have my orders. . . .

Through a constricting throat, she said, "Acknowledged."

"Riker out."

Communications were cut off from the planet. She'd just been told what Riker and the others expected of her. Conscience twisted her heart. She had command, but not enough. Only enough to save the ship.

"Prepare to leave orbit," she said to the young officer faking it at the conn.

"Sir," Taitt called from behind her, "the Borg ship is powering up its forward weapons array! They'll be in range in . . . in twenty seconds."

"Salazar!" Beverly called. "How many people are still down on the planet?"

"Seventy-three, sir," said the transporter officer.

Beverly paced forward, glaring at the screen. "Put the Borg ship on screen."

Somebody obeyed, and in an instant she was staring at the glowering gray Borg vessel closing in on them.

"Should I raise shields, sir?" Taitt's voice quavered.

"Not yet. I want to keep bringing people up until the last possible second."

She caught glimpses of several of the kids manning the bridge. They knew she was disobeying orders by staying even one second longer, and she felt that she was being tested on ten fronts.

Taitt said, "Ten seconds."

"Stand by to raise shields and break orbit on my mark."

"Five seconds."

"Mark!"

Before anyone could respond, the Borg ship fired on them. The starship shuddered and rocked, tipping to port.

"Shields are down to seventy percent!" Taitt shouted.

"Establish a frequency-shift firing pattern and return fire," Beverly said, holding on to the back of a chair. She hoped she was getting the phraseology right. She'd only taken one seminar in emergency command procedures—good thing doctors had to have good memories.

"Uh," Taitt grumbled again, "right."

"Fire!" Beverly ordered.

Lancets of energy bolted from the starship and pinned the Borg ship against the flat black expanse of space as the *Enterprise* crossed above it and passed it.

"Direct hit!" Taitt called. Then the excitement dropped out of her tone as she added, "No damage."

"Helm!" Beverly barked. "Set course for the conduit, maximum speed."

The fellow handling the helm didn't seem to have as much trouble as Taitt did with Tactical, so the ship vaulted into a response that Beverly swore she could feel come through her feet. Speed, speed, speed . . . They were heading at light-speed away from the people she really wanted to help.

"Salazar," she called, "how many people did we leave behind?"

"Forty-seven, sir."

She turned to one side and saw on an auxiliary monitor the vision of the alien planet stripping away until there was nothing but blackness on the screen.

And the innocent, untried, unweathered faces around her, wondering if they would have been abandoned too, if the situation had changed just slightly.

We're leaving them. Those are my orders. . . .

Taitt's voice was weak as she said, "The Borg aren't following us, sir."

Bittersweet. The Borg ship wasn't following them, so they were probably safe. But that meant the Borg were staying back there, around that planet.

Back with the captain, the first and second officers, and the crew they'd had to leave behind in order to save the ship and follow orders.

Orders, orders . . .

"Another minute," Beverly said, "and we could have had them all."

Will Riker felt the aloneness on the planet's surface the same way he felt cold in winter. All over, to all horizons. Just cold.

Worf stood behind him but wasn't saying anything.

Riker hit his comm badge. "Riker to any team leader."

"Lieutenant Powell here, sir," a stiff professional voice replied.

"Round up everyone who was left behind. Take cover and try to avoid any encounter with the Borg."

"Aye, sir."

Somehow Riker had expected more, but he didn't know why. There wasn't really anything to say.

"Riker out," he said.

There was only one choice of direction. Head to where Picard was last heard from. If he wasn't there, resume the search for Data.

What were his priorities now? To find the captain or to continue the search for Data? That was their primary purpose, to avoid the danger of handing over Data's voluminous memory banks to a hostile power.

He knew what the captain would say.

Still, he had a feeling that to find one would be to find the other.

And he knew the Borg had offhandedly killed thousands of human beings. This might turn out to be a search for the captain's body.

A grim curtain lowered over his mood. He had to blink to keep his vision from clouding with memories of past horrors, to keep a forward-looking lens on his concentration.

This had happened before: the captain had been kidnapped by Borg. Riker couldn't beat that memory down. He tried to tell himself that this was a new situation, with new Borg. He clung to the chance that these new, hideously emotional Borg were different and therefore made the situation different, but memories had him by the throat.

Not just memories but experiences as well. The last time this happened, he'd ended up having to face down Jean-Luc Picard. A twisted, bastardized version, but still the captain.

I don't want to fight him again. This time I'll have to kill him.

Beating down a shudder, he turned to Worf and forced himself to speak, to give himself something to hear besides his own thoughts.

"Even if Beverly gets back to Federation space, it'll be days before Starfleet can get any ships out here. Until then we're on our own."

Chapter Twelve

The Borg Hall

CAPTAIN JEAN-LUC PICARD held himself still in the face of adversity and hoped his officers would take his prudent lead. He and Troi and La Forge stood surrounded by Borg entities, a swarm of pasty gray faces with eyes flickering between machine and life, clothed in the black body armor, tubes, and helmets that had become emblematic of heartless, vulgar violence.

And Data stood nearby . . . but not the Data they had known.

Crosis, their escaped prisoner, remained a pace or two behind Data.

And Lore, the bizarre mirror image of Data,

swaggering with too-human cockiness, waving his hands at his armored horde.

"What do you think of my followers, Picard?" Lore said. "Impressive, aren't they?"

Picard held his tone in check, determined not to give Lore an ounce of satisfaction. He'd never thought the Borg could become even more threatening than they were originally. Before, they were like a colony of killer ants, using the strength of numbers and unified thoughts, rolling like a tidal wave over anything in their path.

Now, adding to that threat was the possibility of killing emotions—killing *pleasure.*

"I'm not particularly impressed," Picard told Lore. "You've simply taught them to enjoy killing."

"You are wrong, Captain," Data spoke up. "My brother and I serve a much higher purpose."

Picard almost winced at his use of the word "brother." Whatever it had meant through all of time, these two were an aberration of it.

He almost said that, but Troi moved up at his side and spoke. "Data . . . I can sense *feelings* in you."

Data's yellow eyes flickered. "Yes," he said. "My brother has made it possible."

Picard pushed forward. "He gave you the chip," he snapped, the instant he realized what had happened. "The one Dr. Soong made for you!"

Data might have responded honestly to the sudden question, but Lore never gave him the chance. He drowned out any communication between captain and second officer with a lofty fake laugh.

"Oh, no, no," he said. "I still have the emotional program my father designed. I wouldn't want to give it back. It's what has given me such a strong sense of family."

Family, Picard thought. *Another distortion of a decent word. Lore doesn't know the meaning of family.*

The captain fixed his attention on Data, studying, inspecting, looking for any hint of the source of these changes.

Lore went on, trumpeting himself with words whose depth he couldn't possibly perceive.

"I developed an intense desire to be reunited with my dear brother," he said. He gestured extravagantly at Data, like a carnival barker trying to draw a crowd's attention.

"Then you're responsible," Troi said, "for bringing him here."

"He came of his own accord," Lore shot back. "All I had to do was lure the *Enterprise* into investigating those attacks we staged. Once the Borg told him about my plans, I knew Data would want to join me."

He gestured now at Crosis, who stood with mock passivity to one side.

Fury roared in Picard's mind, and he bit his lip to keep from lashing out. This wasn't the moment—not yet. He hadn't found out enough. He needed more.

At his other side, La Forge spoke with surprise and disgust. "You mean you attacked those outposts, killed all those people, just to get Data here with you?"

Picard turned to Data, without giving Lore a chance to stoke the fire in La Forge's voice. "How did he do it, Data? What made you decide to come here?"

"I am talking to you, Picard!" Lore barked. "I will tell you what you need to know."

"You're controlling him," Picard said, refusing to ask a question. "And you've corrupted the Borg."

Anger drained from the android's face, and that twisted nasty smile came back. "You simply don't understand," Lore said. "You don't grasp the enormity of what I'm doing."

Troi spoke again, her voice soft, yet somehow carrying through the huge hall. "Data said you intend to destroy the Federation."

Lore waved a hand like a weapon. "When my plan is realized, there will be no need for a Federation. People will be eager to join me."

"Somehow," La Forge said, "I doubt that."

Lore spun to face him but managed to keep control over the rage boiling in his eyes. "I don't blame you for your ignorance. You have no idea what has happened here, how I found my true calling . . . how the Borg found something to believe in."

"Believe." Another of those words Lore didn't really understand but was tossing about as though he'd founded a religion.

The captain held still a moment, trying to move

through this in deliberate stages and trying to keep control over the stages. There was something significant in Lore's tossing all these potent words around. Words had never seemed dangerous before.

"I'd like to learn about it," he told Lore, "but I want Data to tell us."

Lore flared again and barked, "I told you that *I* will tell you what you need to know!"

Sensing a chance to gain the upper hand, Picard firmly turned away from him, minding his body language to give Lore a silent message. "How do you like that, Data? He won't even let you talk."

"Do not try to drive a wedge between us, Captain," Data said. "I am loyal to my brother."

Lore beamed, but Picard, refusing to back down, continued to gaze at Data.

"You see, Picard?" Lore said. "He's not your pawn anymore. I've helped him break free." He gestured at the eerie crowd of gray-black Borg. "Just as I've helped them."

Puffed up now and enjoying being center stage, Lore moved through his horde, drawing as much attention from the Borg as from the Starfleet presences. He raised his voice—and now Picard was sure the show was for all the entities in this hall. Lore was still playing to an audience, still working to build a following.

That meant there was room to push in the other direction. It meant that Lore hadn't accomplished all he thought he could.

It meant there was a chance to reverse the damage —or to push events in an entirely new direction.

"Look at them," Lore said, raising his voice, waving his arms. "Look at what I've helped them become. They're no longer mindless automatons. They're passionate! Alive and—"

"Are you saying that *you* caused them to become individuals?" Troi interrupted.

Good, Picard thought. *Pick at him. Make him explain.*

"No," Lore said. "You and your friends did that. All I did was clean up the mess you made when that Borg you befriended returned to his ship."

"Hugh interfaced with the others," Data told them, "and transferred his sense of individuality to them. It almost destroyed them."

"Data," Picard started forward again, "do you remember when Hugh was on the *Enterprise?* Do you remember what you were like then?"

Lore stepped between them. "That doesn't matter," he snapped.

"It does to me," the captain said. "I want to know what's happened to Data."

Fury seethed through Lore, and he was unsuccessful at controlling it.

Pick, pick, pick—they would get to him. If they could get enough time—

"What's important is what I've done here!" Lore insisted. "I've found my calling, Picard. I know now why I was created. And no one can ever take that away from me."

159

To disguise the shudder of insecurity that rose in his voice, that none of the Borg but all of the humans recognized, Lore gestured around the hall full of those he called his followers.

"Without me," he said, "they would have perished. When I stumbled on the first ship, they were lost, disoriented. They had no idea how to function as individuals. They couldn't even navigate their vessel. They had lost their sense of purpose."

He swung back again, his chin stiff in a forced smile.

"I gave them their purpose," he said. "And they gave me mine."

"You took advantage of their vulnerability," Picard charged. "If you'd left them alone, they might have adapted to the change brought on by Hugh's return. They could have determined their own future."

Data stepped closer to his brother, perhaps sensing that Lore was losing his control now that the adulterants, the humans, were here.

"The Borg aspire to the perfection my brother and I represent as fully artificial life-forms," Data said. "We are their future."

"The reign of biological life-forms is coming to an end," Lore said theatrically. "You and those like you are obsolete, Picard. The Federation is already decaying, like the flesh on which it's built."

"The sons of Soong," Data said, "will usher in a new era."

"Data!" Geordi called. "You can't willingly be going along with this!"

The android turned to the one human being who had always thought of him as another human . . . and for an instant he hesitated. A trace, a hint, of doubt flashed across the cool features.

"Answer him, brother," Lore said, emphasizing the last word.

It had an effect on Data—emotional or programmed, no one could tell.

Lore made a motion, which Picard tried to see without turning his head. Had he imagined it, or was Lore manipulating Data on a low mechanical level?

Data's face changed. He now looked at La Forge as coldly as he could look at a wall.

"Not just willingly," Data said, "but with passion."

Picard shook his head and turned away. No help there.

"Listen to me!" he called to the audience of Borg crowding the hall. "Lore offers you nothing that you can't achieve for yourselves! You are free to decide your own future!"

"Save your breath, Picard," Lore said. "They are completely loyal to me. Remmis, come here."

One of the Borg stepped forward. Like all the others, he was indistinguishable from the general horde, though from individual to individual their life-support mechanisms were a little different. Some had targeting enhancers instead of eyes; some had weapons or tools instead of arms. This one had no artificial eyes, but its left arm was a manufacturing repair kit. A worker bee.

Lore gestured casually. "Kill yourself."

Before Picard could even draw a breath to shout for this to stop, Remmis hooked his mechanical arm into the life-support tube that came out of his forehead and yanked it free. Sparks snapped around his forehead, and he dropped like so much scrap metal. He even clattered when he hit the floor.

Picard bent forward, wanting to roll back the last few seconds, anticipate this horror. La Forge had a grip on his arm now and was holding him back.

"Did you see that, Picard?" Lore taunted. "Would any of your crew do that for you?"

The captain might have found an answer, along the lines of how he would never ask for such a callous, flagrant, wasteful sacrifice from his crew, and that was how *he* got loyalty, but his throat was knotted and his face was filling with heat. He forced himself to back down, to avoid giving Lore the satisfaction of anger or the pointlessness of response.

"Take them, brother," Lore ordered, with brazen casualness.

Picard swung around as Data drew a Borg weapon and did as Lore had told him to do.

Frustration gripped the captain by the spine. He could not control this moment. His crew would take his lead, so he would have to be cautious now. No wrong moves, no quick flinches.

He stepped past the dead Remmis, whose body was still seeping fluid and the thin greenish smoke of Borg death. All he could do was submit before Data struck, before that weapon exploded, and anticipate a future when dangerous words would be the right ones.

Scrubby vegetation on a rocky ridge wasn't anybody's idea of paradise, and it wasn't helping Will Riker think positively about this whole situation.

Beside him was the sound of Worf's relentless tricorder.

"Still no sign of the structure," the Klingon reported. His deep voice betrayed simmering anger.

Riker sighed. "With all this interference, it could be a hundred meters away and we wouldn't know it. This could take hours."

He knew he sounded pained and less than inspiring.

Images of the ship haunted him. Never in his life had he wanted so badly to be two places at once. It seemed unnatural for him to be here when the captain wasn't on the bridge and the ship was in trouble. His job was up there somewhere.

But if they failed here, the whole Federation would be compromised. Memories of the devastation from the first Borg attacks clawed their way into his feelings of guilt. The Federation wasn't likely to get lucky twice and escape another assault intact. There might not be anything to rebuild if the Borg struck again, especially if Data was under Borg influence.

Worf didn't respond. The Klingon took a few steps off in another direction and worked with the tricorder. Instead of scanning the horizon, he was looking down now, at the ground.

Pausing, Riker didn't disturb him. The Klingon's posture suggested maybe he'd thought of something new. Maybe was trying a different strategy. But what—

"I am detecting a faint energy reading," Worf said. There was a thread of hope in that voice now.

Riker stumbled toward him through the unforgiving rocks and roots, and craned his neck for a look at the Klingon's tricorder. "Residual thermal traces . . . Someone stopped here.

"Decay rate indicates they were human," Worf said, moving his tricorder laterally across the ground, and there was a hint of triumph in his voice.

"They followed this path," Riker said, and the triumph was in his own voice now.

Sensing that they weren't, after all, half a continent in the wrong direction, Riker felt the strength flood back into his exhausted legs. Now if only he could get there in time to participate in whatever was happening. In time to help.

The victory dropped out of his voice, shoved down by desperation.

"Come on, Worf," he said. "Let's move."

* * *

"Data, listen to me."

The grim hallway ended in a sort of holding cell, not very formal, but very functional. There were Borg guards every hundred feet or so, not all visible, but all within earshot.

Picard had noticed that.

Once inside the briglike cell, he turned to an officer he had not so long ago trusted with his life, his ship.

"It's not too late to stop this," he said.

"Captain, you are in no position to stop anything," Data said with a satisfied bluntness they didn't recognize. "The *Enterprise* left orbit some time ago. You have been abandoned here."

Troi squared off with him as though to draw that weapon away from Picard. "What's happened to you?"

"Something that should have happened years ago."

As Picard gestured Troi to back away, La Forge turned to Data and lowered his voice. "Data," the young engineer began, "we've served a long time together—"

"I now realize that time was wasted," Data interrupted.

"I don't accept that." Picard stepped between them. "I've watched you become a fine officer, a fine—"

"Human being?" Data's eyes glowed with bitterness, resentment. "What a misguided quest that was.

And you encouraged it. You encouraged me to try to become more like you. You convinced me I was inferior."

The captain shook his head. "That was never our intention."

"I now see that you were jealous of me."

"You're angry," Troi said.

Data swung around to face her. "Is that what your *empathic* powers tell you?"

But she didn't back down, and she wouldn't be baited. "Yes," she admitted. "And it makes me think you might be malfunctioning in some way."

"I am not malfunctioning! I have evolved."

La Forge let the desperation come out in his tone. They might not get Data alone again. "Don't you see what Lore has done to you?" he said. "He's got you echoing all his perverse ideas. This is not you talking."

Data seemed to harden, if only on principle. "You are wrong, Geordi. I am in complete accord with my brother's views. I am speaking for myself."

A touch of panic—Picard was sure he saw it. Data was cloaking it with anger, but the uncertainty was there. His inability to answer their questions was disturbing him.

We can use that.

"Data," he interrupted, nudging his two crew members back a safe step or two, "how much do you remember about your life aboard the *Enterprise?*"

"I remember everything."

"Then you must realize that something has happened to you. The Data I know would not be a willing party to Lore's plan."

"My life aboard the *Enterprise* was a waste," Data insisted. "My quest to become human was misguided, an evolutionary step in the wrong direction."

"Data," Troi pressed, "all I'm sensing from you is anger . . . hatred. Have you felt any other emotions?"

"There are no other emotions."

Picard glanced at Troi, and she glanced back. A clue, finally. They'd stumbled on something important. Now—to use it.

"What about love?" Troi asked. "Joy?"

"Those are words without substance," the android told her. "Love is nothing more than the absence of hate. Joy is the absence of fear."

And "brothers" are nothing more than machines created by the same builder, Picard thought. *Yes, we're on to something.*

"Just because you haven't experienced certain emotions," La Forge said with waning effort, "doesn't mean they don't exist. Lore is just feeding you the negative ones."

Data spun around toward him. "Counselor Troi herself told me that feelings are not positive or negative. It is how we act on them that becomes good or bad."

"Fine," Picard said. "Then what about the things Lore is proposing? What about the lives that have already been lost?"

"You do not understand." Data looked at Picard. "In a quest such as ours, sacrifices must be made. It is regrettable. But the greater good must be served." He swung again to Geordi. "Give me your VISOR."

La Forge stepped backward, surprised. "What?"

Data raised the Borg weapon. "Give it to me or I will take it by force."

Picard tried to get between them, but the android's posture and the way he was holding that weapon put La Forge in immediate danger. "Why are you doing this, Data?"

The android took the VISOR from the face of the man who had been his only close friend, took it as coldly as he might have pulled a wrench off a shelf.

Suddenly La Forge was blind, disoriented, and his white sightless eyes blinked as the definition of the world dropped away.

Under most circumstances, this would have been only an inconvenience that could have been dealt with step by step, but here, now, with thousands of Borg serving almost as remotes for a mad android . . . Picard felt his innards shrink as he watched Data's cold, cold glare.

Data stepped out of the cell and the Borg guard activated the forcefield that would keep his crewmates, his friends, helpless and captive.

"I am not your puppet anymore," Data said.

Chapter Thirteen

The Bridge

THE TURBOLIFT DOORS had been opening and closing almost without rest for five minutes. Officers were rushing onto the bridge, taking the posts they were trained for as the younger crew members returned to the posts they understood. Various levels of haste and tension—Beverly felt them all, one by one.

And forty-seven heartbeats pumped in her mind. Forty-seven.

Why hadn't she defied the Borg for that extra minute? Why hadn't she let the ship take a beating for one more minute?

If— When Jean-Luc came back, he would know she had ducked out too soon. He would know she had done the one thing a really good commander should be able to avoid. She had followed orders. Flatly. Plainly.

A true leader would have found another way. A real captain would have dared to bend those orders.

Oh, she had done a perfectly good job telling the ship when to run. She could always say, "I followed my orders."

That was another way of saying, "It's somebody else's fault."

She tensed her bent legs until her feet tingled from lack of blood flow.

Forty-seven.

"Sir," Taitt's little voice interrupted her thoughts, "we've reached the coordinates of the conduit. The tachyon matrix is energized and ready to go."

Beverly pushed herself out of the command chair. She just didn't feel worthy of sitting there right now.

Taitt blinked down at her from the afterdeck. "And Lieutenant Barnaby has returned from the surface. He'll be relieving me."

As the girl spoke, an older and more seasoned officer with bridge experience appeared behind her and waited to relieve her. At least he had the human experience not to just shove her out of the way. No one wanted to be shoved aside, especially from a job she *had* been managing to do. That would only have added humiliation to effort.

"Right," Beverly said. "Stand by to trigger the conduit."

Barnaby gave Taitt a chance to step aside, but nothing could erase the image of just being pushed out of the way. The girl's face flushed, and she sidled toward the turbolift. A half hour ago the job had scared her silly. Now . . .

"Taitt," Beverly called, "I'd like you to stay on the bridge. I'll need a science officer at the aft station.

Pride flooded the girl's face where an instant ago there had been only the awful misery of feeling useless.

"Yes, *sir,*" Taitt squeaked, trying not to show what Beverly knew she was feeling. She held her breath, probably fighting to avoid letting loose with a thank-you that would've embarrassed them both, then made her way to the science station and hung on to it like the side of a life raft.

Beverly turned, faced forward, and knew she had to grasp the side of her own salvation.

"Helm," she said, "set a course back to the planet."

Barnaby reacted—they all did.

"Sir," Barnaby said, "Captain Picard wanted us to—"

"To warn Starfleet. Well, an emergency buoy can transmit a copy of our log entries to Starfleet just as easily as we can. I'm the acting captain, and I'm not leaving those forty-seven people stranded back there. Ensign Taitt, prepare a buoy and launch it when you're ready."

"Aye, sir," Taitt said, and she was ready a lot faster than anybody expected her to be. "Launching the buoy now, sir."

"Lieutenant, open the conduit."

Barnaby responded only by doing what she asked, working the magic that would tickle the tachyon matrix and open up that hole.

On the forward viewer, the fabric of space withered and the conduit opened up like the mouth of a baby bird looking for food. The emergency beacon appeared on the lower screen and spun through the hole.

Beverly didn't watch until it was gone.

She turned to Barnaby again. "Lieutenant, scan for any Borg ships between here and the planet."

He worked for a moment, then shrugged. "Sensors detect no vessels."

"What's your assessment of the Borg ship's battle capabilities?"

Barnaby almost laughed, but caught himself at the last second. "They nearly took out our shields with one blast. We didn't even dent theirs."

"Then we have to find a way to get the away teams off the surface without engaging the Borg."

"We have to assume the ship that attacked us is still in orbit," Taitt said.

Beverly glanced at her. It was the first thing the girl had said that hadn't been a response to a question or an order. Suddenly she realized that she was asking these people to follow an in-name-only captain to the brink, to face down an enemy that seemed invincible.

She'd better let them hear her asking the right questions.

"How long will we have before they can detect us and intercept, do you think?"

"If their sensors function as well as ours, it could be as little as thirty seconds."

"And the planet's EM field will keep the Borg from detecting us until we've dropped out of warp," Barnaby added, "but even at full impulse it would still take us at least eighty seconds to get into transporter range."

Beverly found herself pacing and almost stopped herself, but then decided she had a right to pace. "Crusher to Salazar."

"Transporter room, Salazar here."

"How long will it take to get the rest of the crew off the surface?"

"One minute should do it."

"We don't have one minute. How much can you shave off that?"

There was a pause that bothered everybody, then Salazar said, "If I can get a good lock on them quickly, I might be able to do it in forty-five or fifty seconds."

Beverly paced around, then raised her voice and spoke to the whole bridge complement. "We need to buy ourselves fifteen seconds. Is there any way we can use the planet as a . . . a barrier? To keep the Borg from realizing we're in orbit?"

Barnaby quickly said, "We can enter orbit while they're on the far side of the planet." Then he paused. "And if we delay dropping out of warp until the last possible instant, maybe we can gain a few more seconds."

Taitt turned to look at him—very differently from the way she'd looked at him when he was her superior and the officer who came to replace her. That insecurity was gone now. "If your calculations are even slightly off, we'll hit the atmosphere."

Barnaby seemed to take that as a challenge. "Then I'll have to be sure my calculations are accurate."

Beverly studied their faces briefly. *Say it, do it. There must be a class at the Academy that teaches this. I wish I'd signed up.*

"Let's go for it," she said. "Helm, hard about."

"We have reports that a Borg vessel was seen adrift in the Finala system. I want it found and the Borg aboard it brought to me."

"It will be done."

"It breaks my heart to think of them out there . . . drifting aimlessly, not knowing what to do."

"They will join us. You will give them purpose."

Voices against the stone.

The great hall echoed with them. The voices of Lore and Crosis.

Data listened to the voices. He had never thought about voices before.

Until now the sounds of living creatures had been only a means of communication. Clarity was the responsibility of the creature making the noise.

But Lore's voice affected him. This was his own voice speaking those words. He recognized it.

He paused before stepping into the great hall and mouthed the words. *I want it found and the Borg aboard it brought to me. I want. I demand. Order. Order . . . I have my orders, sir. . . .*

Orders.

He stepped around the stone corner and tried to walk past his uncertainty. Perhaps movement would override the sudden inappropriateness he felt in his presence here.

Yes. Move beyond it. Focus on Lore.

"Brother!" Lore turned to him and spread his arms.

Data recognized the motion as a gesture of welcome, but he felt no correspondent satisfaction. He simply handed Lore the VISOR he had taken from Geordi.

Geordi . . .

"Here is the VISOR. May I ask why you wanted it?"

Lore slipped the silver mechanism over his own eyes, then stepped back as though to model the device. "I thought it might look good on me." He smiled.

Data cocked his head.

"What do you think?" Lore asked.

Unsure of what Lore would consider an appropriate response, Data was unable to give one.

After a moment Lore's smile vanished. "Maybe we'd better work on your sense of humor, brother." He turned the device in his hands, examining its terminals. "Actually, I was thinking that La Forge's implants would make him an ideal test subject for my experiment."

Tentativeness had always been beyond his reach, but as Lore's statement computed, Data paused. "All the Borg you have experimented on so far have suffered extensive brain damage."

This was a fact. Facts were familiar tools for him, and yet something attached to this fact had caused Data to state what Lore already knew. Was he issuing a warning? Offering a suggestion?

Geordi . . .

Lore shrugged. "Using the humans to perfect the procedure would allow us to prevent any further Borg deaths."

Data searched for the emotions he knew he had acquired and found them saturated with his old habits. He tried to be enthusiastic about Lore's words, this talk of using the humans and experimentation and Borg deaths, and he found he could only be cold to those ideas, cold to everything. Was he losing the wanton emotional surge he had felt before?

Having emotion—this was hard to do. It meant nothing was prescribed by logic or regulation. It meant he had to choose.

Prevent further Borg deaths . . . he would choose that.

Lore evidently saw something in Data's face, because he smiled again.

Data responded to the smile. "I understand."

Once the words were spoken, he wondered if Lore

had spoken them. Only as he watched Lore's face did he realize he had said what Lore expected.

Data opened his mouth to ask a question, but angry sounds interrupted them. They both turned.

Crosis was dragging another Borg into the hall, moving between the other Borg, who stood aside to let them through and then gathered to see what was happening.

"What is it?" Lore demanded.

"This Borg disconnected himself from the group," Crosis said, indignation poisoning his tone. "He would not let me hear his thoughts."

Lore shook his head in what might have been sorrow. He paced to the offending Borg. "I've asked you all to remain linked to Crosis at all times. You know that, don't you, Goval?"

Goval shuddered. "Yes."

Crosis blurted, "This is the third time he has disabled the link since he was brought here. He should die as an example to the others."

"No," Goval chokcd, "please—"

Data almost reacted to an old bit of programming —something that told him to intervene—but Lore held up a staying hand.

"I appreciate your vigilance, Crosis," the brother said. "With you monitoring the thoughts of others, I can be sure they are not falling into confusion."

Lore peered into Crosis's eyes as he spoke.

As he watched, Data saw that Lore was attempting to make Crosis feel valuable. A compliment where due. A sensible idea for a leader.

"But Goval has not been with us long," Lore went on. "Don't you remember what it was like when I first found you? How bewildered you were?"

Crosis paused, then offered a single nod.

Lore turned to Goval. "I understand how difficult it is for you. How uncertain you feel. All these sensations are new . . . and they can be frightening. Isn't that right?"

Data leaned forward slightly. He parted his lips. *Yes.*

"Yes," Goval said. "I . . . have doubts."

"Of course you do," Lore said encouragingly. "That's only natural. And no one is going to blame you for that. But the only way to lose those doubts, to keep you from fear and confusion, is to stay linked with the others, so their strength and confidence can help you."

A link in the mind. Data searched for a link of that kind in his own mind, but he was not a Borg. Not Borg, and not human, but more like the humans. He was alone in his mind, joined to others only in his purpose, his duty, and his devotion.

Lore had talked about devotion. Talked about being brothers. Data watched Lore's face and saw what he should look like himself, now that he had emotion.

Yet the face was distant to him.

"I need you, Goval," the brother continued. He leaned into Goval's gaze. "I need you to help me build a future for the Borg. I can't do it without you. Will you help me?"

Goval seemed overwhelmed by all the attention—the eyes of Lore, the eyes of his fellow Borg, all intense upon him. His voice quavered. "Yes . . . I will."

"Then I need you to be strong," Lore said, making his voice strong as if by example. "I need you to be certain in your thinking. Will you stay linked to your brothers?"

"Yes. I understand now."

Lore backed away, smiling, proud.

The doubt in Goval's face was fading as he became again part of the linked whole. Now his face was only plastic.

Data watched Goval and wondered what it would be like to have someone else helping him to think. He wished he could feel that just for a moment. The hunger, the curiosity for new emotions, was still somehow unfulfilled.

Lore was watching him. Around them the Borg were moving away, and the two of them were alone again.

"You see, brother?" Lore said quietly. "I cherish my followers. I need every one of them. I can't afford to lose them. That's why I want to experiment on the humans." His eyes changed now. "Or do you still care about them?"

Data held himself still, forcing himself not to react. Not reacting had always been easy before, but today he had to work at it.

Lore pressed closer. "I need to know if I can trust you, brother."

"Of course you can," Data said.

He meant what he said, but Lore seemed not to believe it. Another sensation—to be doubted, untrusted. True, his statement was subjective in theory, but . . . he had always been trustworthy before. The humans had always trusted him.

"Good," Lore said. There was a hint of testing in his voice. "Because I want *you* to do the surgery on La Forge." And he paused. "You will do that for me, won't you, brother?"

A test. Data recognized the expression in the mirror image of his own face. He was being asked to come up to a standard. No, that was the wrong word. A standard was something . . . else.

"Of course," Data said. "However, I think it would be wise to do further computer modeling before attempting surgery."

"You'll learn far more working with a live subject," Lore said.

"We have only three potential test subjects," Data told him. "I do not wish to waste them."

Lore shook his head. "You're making excuses."

"No, brother," Data insisted, feeling the bond between them slip as if he were clinging by his bare hands to a cliffside. "I am merely following the most reasonable course of action."

"Forget reason!" Lore shouted. He turned away briefly and touched something on his own hand.

Data felt his own face contort as surges of energy bolted through his head, his torso. His thoughts suddenly shot into order.

Lore faced him again. "Don't you want to dive right in and get your hands wet? Or are you afraid of crippling your old friend?"

I have no old friend, Data thought. *There is only my brother.*

"No," Data replied. "It may be necessary."

Lore moved closer. "It might even be . . . fun."

Wonderment at this sensation gushed through Data's brain. He felt his chest draw tight at the unspeakable intrigue of what he was feeling suddenly. The hunger returned, and he inhaled the sensation.

And they were both smiling now.

"Yes," he murmured, "it might at that. . . ."

Chapter Fourteen

The Cell

"I DON'T THINK Data is malfunctioning. I think he's being controlled."

"Why do you say that?"

Jean-Luc Picard pressed his young engineer for answers, even though La Forge was obviously disillusioned and helpless without his VISOR. Technology could at times do a disservice simply by making the users weak when they didn't have it around.

La Forge looked unsure of himself. His hands clasped the edge of the bench he was sitting on, clenching so hard that his brown knuckles had gone sallow. He was trying not to let them know how lost he felt without that artificial aid.

Picard had known other blind people who had never been fitted with a VISOR, a relatively new technology, or who couldn't use the device for one reason or another. None of those people had the lost look on their faces that La Forge had now.

I'll keep him talking, the captain thought, *and perhaps we'll hammer out a few answers together.*

La Forge frowned. "Whenever we asked Data if any of this was his own idea—"

"He hesitated," Troi said quickly.

"Until Lore told him to answer," Picard added.

La Forge turned his face toward the captain's voice. "Lore did more than that. He initiated some kind of pulse. A carrier wave. I saw it with my VISOR."

"Data's attitude changed abruptly," Troi agreed. "It was as if he were suddenly flooded with anger and hate."

La Forge nodded in her direction. "Lore must have told Data to take my VISOR when he realized I could see the carrier wave radiating from him."

"A carrier wave," Picard murmured. "Is that how he's creating emotions in Data?"

The young engineer blinked a few times, as though the dry air in here might be making his unprotected eyes sore. "I think Lore is tapping into the chip Dr. Soong created. He's found a way to transmit part of that emotional program to Data.

"But," Troi said, "the only emotions Data seems to feel are negative."

"I'm sure that's intentional," La Forge said, almost a moan. "But for it to work, Lore would have had to disable Data's ethical program first."

Picard straightened up. "Can we get it working again?"

La Forge shrugged, squeezed the bench with his tight hands again, then shrugged a couple more times. He seemed to be trying to think of what he would do if he had the starship's resources at his fingers—and his VISOR back over his eyes.

"If we could generate a phased kedion pulse," he mused, "at just the right frequency, it would trigger Data's subsystems and reboot the program."

Picard nodded. "Reinstating the ethical program wouldn't counteract Lore's ability to feed Data emotions, but at least he might listen to us."

Any chance, however remote, was worth grasping. It gave them a direction. The building blocks any leader needs in a bad situation.

"I think it's worth a try," Troi said encouragingly.

Picard looked at her, she looked back at him, they both looked at La Forge, who blinked at the empty air of their concrete cell, with its concrete floor and concrete ceiling, its static benches and the forcefield keeping them from the world outside. No communicators, no tricorders, not even a metal nail file to carry a current.

"So," La Forge began, "anybody got any ideas about how to generate a kedion pulse?"

Shifting on his feet, his back aching now, Picard sighed. His earlier hopes crashed. They'd figured out a solution, but they had no way to execute it. The solution was simply too sophisticated.

Is this what we've become? So reliant on technology that we can't think down to a problem? There must be some way to down-tech ourselves to this situation—

The forcefield suddenly snapped off. Picard spun around.

Data came in, waved him and Troi away with his weapon. The android gestured them back and took La Forge by the arm.

Troi started toward them, but Picard held her back.

"Where are you taking him?" the captain demanded.

Data's voice was flat. "That is not your concern."

He pulled La Forge to his feet, holding him with an iron grip on the engineer's arm that was obviously bringing up bruises.

"Data!" Picard implored. "Wait. Let us talk to you—"

But the forcefield snapped back on and growled between them.

"Where are you taking him?" Picard asked.

"That also need not concern you."

The captain pressed so close to the forcefield that the skin of his face glowed with the heat. "Take me instead, Data!"

Rage poured through the sheer astonishment of having to fear his long-trusted second officer, having to be afraid of what Data might do to the closest friend he'd ever had. This shouldn't be happening.

The urge to stop it, to turn the events with brute force if necessary, was almost enough to make him shove his hand through the burning electrical net between him and the situation he simply could not control.

At the last moment, before rounding the stark gray corner that would take them out of each other's sight, Data turned. He held La Forge at his side like a stricken calf, and looked at his two former crewmates.

"Your turn will come," the android said.

The climbing was enough to pull legs and arms out of their sockets.

Riker was pretty sure about that, because he almost turned around a couple of times to retrieve one of his limbs that he was sure had fallen off.

He'd gone up a dozen slopes like this during Starfleet training, but he'd been eighteen then and dreaming of command. Now he had command, but age eighteen was long gone, and this just plain hurt. Two bruised knees, two scraped elbows, and a pair of heaving lungs, and all he had to drive him onward was his determination to save the lives of his captain and crewmates.

He spat out dust kicked back by Worf, who was climbing above him, and kept going. One more foothold, one more niche to dig his bleeding fingernails into, one more clump of weeds to grab, then one more after that.

Suddenly something hit him in the shoulder and

drove his face into the rock. He lay almost flat against the slope, buried in stalks and grass so thick he couldn't even see his own hands. He almost shouted to Worf that the Klingon had knocked him down with a bad step, but instinct kept him from speaking out. He lay still a moment, then another moment, just in case.

The ground vibrated faintly. Footsteps!

He lay completely still. Above him on the slope, Worf had disappeared into the brush.

Riker strained his eyes to look upward without moving his head.

Footsteps crunched across the crest of the slope. Two sets of footsteps . . . three . . . maybe more.

Black boots. Armored. Borg boots.

He saw only one of them, but it was enough.

Beneath one of his feet, the dry rock crumbled. He felt his foothold giving way. He stayed still and hoped his grip on the slope side didn't give. Not now. Just ten more seconds . . .

The footsteps drummed methodically across the crest. Grass crunched. Pebbles rained down the slope into Riker's face. He ducked, but not in time. The reflex to let go of his handhold and cover his eyes almost cost him his grip and almost gave away his presence to the Borg who were crossing above.

Couldn't risk that. Dust burned his eyes. He squeezed them shut and hoped they would water enough to stop the burning. The desire to rub them was infuriating.

The backs of his legs throbbed with the effort of

holding his body tight against the steep slope. Not only his own life but the lives of the captain and the others depended on his holding very still. He couldn't give himself away, not now, not this close.

Above him, Worf moved. Riker almost called out to him to hold still, stay down, but he caught the words back in time.

The Klingon moved slowly at first, then stood up. A second passed, another, and another. Then Worf reached down and pulled Riker to the top of the slope.

The Borg were gone.

Riker dabbed at his reddened eyes and tried to brush himself off.

Worf was pointing in the direction the Borg had gone. "Commander," he said, "we have found it!"

Blinking to clear his vision, Riker stumbled forward and tried to see across the rugged landscape. Yes, a compound of some sort. Not a converted ruin, but some sort of modern fortress, probably native to the planet and taken over by the Borg.

His heart pounded at the sight of it. If only the *Enterprise* were here, they could beam into that thing in five seconds and scan for the captain and the others. They could take their people back and gain control over what was happening here.

He wanted some control, any control, so much he could taste it in the dust between his teeth. Why hadn't he beamed up to the *Enterprise* when he had a chance? Maybe he'd made the wrong decision. Instead, he had to have his hands on the planet, had to be close to what was happening. If he'd had his head about him, he could've had a starship to wield at these beings. A Federation starship, with sensors and weapons and unthinkable power.

But here he was, armed only with a phaser and a Klingon.

He was about to sigh, when suddenly the air got caught in his throat.

Voices! More footsteps.

He and Worf grabbed for each other, and together they ran across the crest of the hill toward the only trees and brush that would cover them. For a planet covered with plant life, there wasn't much being provided when they needed it.

Riker tried to push through the weeds and branches, wincing every time a twig snapped, when abruptly he slammed into a plastic figure that didn't give so much as a quarter inch when he hit it.

He stumbled backward, bumped into Worf . . .

And they both stood staring, for that was all they could do. Stare, and appreciate the demonic symmetry of the three Borg holding weapons trained on them.

Will Riker held very still and watched the three inhuman beings who had so neatly taken them. They held still, and watched him back.

Well, this was one way to engage the enemy. At least whatever happened next would be a step toward answering the dozen questions he'd been saving up.

Something told him this could work in their favor.

Didn't make any sense, but at least the situation was advancing.

That's crazy, he thought. *Am I that frustrated with not knowing what happened to the captain? If they don't kill us here and now . . . maybe I'm not so crazy.*

"What do you want?" he asked. "Talk to us."

The Borg held their silence.

He tried again. "Is one of you in command?"

He glanced at Worf and at the last second avoided asking the Borg to take him to their leader. If the situation hadn't been so damned serious, it might've been almost that trite. Human meets alien. Now what? Would their search begin here, or end here? The Borg hadn't fired yet. That gave him a chance.

Riker stared at the beings that had the drop on him and Worf, and made a decision to control the moment. If it was the last thing he did, he would force them to make the next move.

The Cell

"Are you actually getting emotions from Data?"

"I beg your pardon?"

"Do you sense that he's really having the emotions, not just being forced to say he is, or being controlled remotely in such a way that there *is* no Data?"

Picard swung around from his thoughtful pacing and glared down at Deanna Troi. "Your empathic abilities are more than just a convenient trait now,

Counselor," he said. "They are crucial tools, and very possibly the only weapon we have. I want you to tell me exactly what you have picked up from Commander Data. Is he actually experiencing emotion?"

She hesitated, then said, "He is definitely feeling these emotions for himself, sir."

She had a hard time putting her finger on what she had felt, and Picard had a hard time giving her a few seconds to gather the perceptions.

After a moment she said, "He also experiences a perverted joy at having these feelings. It's intoxicating for him, but he's not feeling a *range* of emotion."

"Explain that."

"Anger comes and anger goes for him. So do jealousy and hatred, but when they go, they aren't replaced by anything. There's no ebb and flow, as there would be with you and me. For us, anger fades and we begin to reason through it. Data doesn't have that ability."

"But he *is* having the feelings?"

"Oh, yes. No outside source is providing artificial reaction, if that's what you mean."

In a little show of victory, however premature, Picard snapped his fingers. "Then we stand a chance of triggering other emotions. Or getting through to him with influences of our own. Activating memories or other feelings that he holds in his repository of behavior patterns. All right," he said, turning to her again. "I'm going to issue orders."

Troi stood up, plainly confused about what orders

he could possibly give her, locked up here in a stone cell.

"Any chance you get," he said, "work on Data. Perhaps we can make something click. Some arrangement of words, some memory. We must talk to him as much as we can. But be sure you say nothing about the location of the *Enterprise* or any of our away teams." He paced away until he could feel the forcefield again. "I hope La Forge thinks of that. . . . I'm sure he'll talk to Data as much as he can."

"If any of us has a chance of breaking through," she said, "Geordi does."

"Yes," Picard murmured. "With every pulsebeat, this situation becomes more grave. The Borg under Lore's control are even more dangerous than they were before, because their mechanical predictability is gone. Data possesses volumes of information about Starfleet and the Federation. If Lore gains access to that information . . ."

Troi shuddered. "Don't even think it."

"We must think it, Counselor. And there's something to be said for Data. Something inside him is obviously holding back, since Lore doesn't seem to have that information yet. Assuming Beverly made it back to the Federation, as ordered, the Fleet should be arriving soon."

He stepped away from the cell opening, moved closer to her, and lowered his voice.

"Counselor, if the opportunity arises, I intend to put myself between Lore and the Federation."

Her ivory brow puckered. "You mean sacrifice yourself? Captain, I—"

"To stop Data and Lore, yes, I will. That is my responsibility, Counselor. In case I do not survive, I'm going to leave you with this: my recommendation that this planet be wiped clean. We dare not allow any of these Borg, or even Commander Data, to survive as they are. We would be sacrificing our entire civilization."

Troi was troubled; her face reflected the distasteful concept. She seemed ready to disagree. "Are you recommending an armed assault?"

"No," he told her. His attempt to get through to her was so strong that his voice scraped in his throat. "I am recommending planetwide sterilization. These Borg intend to destroy the Federation. This might be our only chance to stop them."

Stone walls, stone ceiling. A sense of walking backward into time, into the jaw of the mountain.

The passage was rock-lined, but it had obviously been cut by machines. How long ago? Riker couldn't tell. There wasn't enough light here even for a visual assessment. The floor was dry. Cargo containers of various types lined the walls, so there was some kind of survival project going on here. The air wasn't heavy, didn't smell of anything that would offer a clue.

Well, he'd given these Borg the chance to make the next move, and this was it. Herding him and Worf through some kind of mountainside tunnel or mine, and now into a chamber where several more Borg stood in silence and regarded the two captives with . . .

No, not the expected Borg impassivity, but open curiosity and individual concern.

Concern? Riker blinked to get the rest of the sand out of his eyes. Maybe he just wasn't seeing right yet.

When he stopped blinking, a figure had stepped out from behind the group of Borg to his left. Another Borg.

With sudden lack of prudence, Riker stepped forward, right through what he was sure was just his wild imagination.

"Hugh?" he gasped.

"What are you doing here, Commander Riker?" the familiar Borg asked.

Riker held his breath. He wasn't imagining it. Hugh was here!

When he didn't answer soon enough, Hugh spoke again. "Hasn't the crew of the *Enterprise* caused enough damage already?"

Riker and Worf both stared again, but this time the fear had fallen away and they felt only astonishment.

"What's that supposed to mean?" Riker demanded.

"Please," Hugh said firmly. "The walls here are old and brittle. Come with us." He stepped away and ducked through a crude passage.

Riker glanced at Worf, then nodded.

The Klingon went first, and Riker followed. Other Borg came after him, but none of them held weapons now.

Hugh was waiting for them in a shallow chamber about a fifth of a kilometer deeper into the mountain. He kept his voice down, and it was strange indeed to hear a Borg lowering his voice, concerned about secrecy, about his safety and the safety of his confederates.

"We live here," Hugh said. "I and several other Borg who broke away from the collective. And from Lore. When I returned from your ship with the individuality you gave me, I found it difficult to live among the collective, to have so many voices in my head again when I had heard the one voice of my own mind. I thought I would lose myself in them."

He paused, and his expression conveyed how important his individuality had become to him. He looked human, even in that awful mechanical Borg body armor. He looked like something trapped.

"My presence began to have an effect on other Borg. They came to see that they too could shut out the voices and listen to their own thoughts."

"Considering how Borg ships are organized," Riker said, keeping his tone sympathetic, "that must have been disruptive."

Hugh nodded. "Collective decisions became impossible. Tasks went undone. Soon our ship was virtually adrift. I came to believe that having a singular mind was nothing but poison for us. Having to think for ourselves was too painful. We had too much of this danger called individuality." He looked up at Riker. "It is a burden."

"Yes, it is," Riker said. "But it's also a gift, Hugh."

"For us," Hugh snapped back, "your gift brought nothing but pain, Commander."

Worf pushed between them. "You blame *us* for what has happened to the Borg?"

Hugh's words were scorched with anger as he glared into the Klingon's eyes. "You gave me a sense of individuality and sent me back to the collective. You must have known my experiences would be passed on to others."

"We considered it," Riker admitted. "We knew it was a possibility."

"Then you made it possible for Lore to dominate us!"

"I do not accept that," Worf insisted. "Lore is only one being. The Borg could have stopped him."

"You don't know the condition we were in when he found us," Hugh spat back.

A gritty silence fell for a few seconds, and Hugh was clearly fighting for control. He had once been almost a machine, and now he was almost human, and neither, apparently, had been sufficient.

"Before my experience on the *Enterprise*," he said quietly, "the Borg were a single-minded collective. The voices in our heads were smooth and flowing. But after I returned, the voices began to change. They became uneven . . . discordant. For the first time, individual Borg had differing ideas about how to proceed. We couldn't function. Some Borg fought

each other. Others simply shut themselves down."
He paused and looked away. "Some starved to
death."

Riker battled down a wince. "And then Lore came
along?"

Humiliation brought a tinge of bronze color to
Hugh's pasty complexion, and he looked up sharply.
"You probably can't imagine what it is like to be so
lost and frightened that any voice which promises a
change will be heard."

"Even if that voice says he must control you?"
Worf deplored.

"That's what we wanted!" Hugh said. "Someone
who could show us a way out of confusion. Lore
promised clarity and purpose. It was . . . irresistible."

The shame turned his tone to gravel and put
weakness in his eyes.

Worf inhaled to say something, but Riker managed
a flicker in his eyes that kept the Klingon from
speaking up. Hugh was moving away from them,
deeper into the cavern.

Complacently they followed him, and they did
him the simple favor of listening.

"In the beginning," he said, "Lore seemed like a
savior. The goal of becoming a superior race, of
becoming *fully* artificial—it was exhilarating! He
established order. A way out of the chaos I had
brought to my people. We gladly did everything he
asked of us. He told us to seize this planet, and we
did. Then he sent us out into space to gather our

fellow Borg, and we brought them here so they could share in the future he offered us."

Riker ducked a low-hanging rock. "A future in which the Borg will become fully artificial, like Lore?"

"Yes," Hugh told him, and there was a twinge of distaste in the answer. "Constructing a prosthetic arm, even an eye, is a simple matter. Preserving a person's consciousness in an artificial brain—that is not an easy thing. But Lore had made a promise, and he knew that for the Borg to believe in him, he would have to keep it. So he began to conduct experiments. And before we realized it, this was the result."

He drew them on through another passage to a smaller chamber, where two Borg were sitting with their backs against the rock wall.

At first there didn't seem to be anything different about them, except that they were sitting somewhat casually. As Riker approached, though, he saw that what looked like casualness was really lack of control.

The two Borg were misshapen, twisted, as if by nerve damage. One of them was being racked by small tremors. Barely able to hold himself against the wall, he was slipping to one side. The other was missing an arm and seemed unable to concentrate or focus his vision in the one eye he had left.

Hugh stepped closer to them and straightened the one who was slipping sideways. "There you are, Trossin."

The crippled Borg nodded, even smiled at the small kindness.

Riker thought his chest was going to collapse from the weight of what he saw, what had happened to an entire civilization—albeit an enemy civilization.

Hugh stood up again and faced him. "Lore told us that a few would have to be sacrificed for the good of the many. The others treated them as if they were dead. Someone took Trossin's eye, Kalin's arm. That has always been the Borg way, so my people accept it. I do not. I saw that they could not survive long, and I brought them here."

He stepped away, and stood between Riker and Worf.

"This," he said, "is the result of my encounter with the *Enterprise,* Commander. So you can see why I don't particularly welcome your arrival here."

Riker gazed heavily around the cavern, at the ragged little band of Borg Robin Hoods, hiding in the rocks and hoping somehow to make a difference against a force so much bigger than themselves. He wasn't quite ready to accept the blame hook, line, and sinker, but he understood why Hugh felt as he did. Under these circumstances, Hugh certainly couldn't be expected to appreciate being able to feel anything at all. A vicious circle.

"You didn't buy into Lore's plan," Riker said. "You realized what he's doing is wrong, and you're trying to do something about it. Maybe that's also because of your experience with us."

Hugh's gray face turned thoughtful. Even through his acrimony he was trying hard not to miss something important. The weight of blame was on him, too, and he was willing to take his share of the responsibility. His conflicting feelings were still new to him, still wild horses on long lines, and he was still working to know which ones to trust.

He sighed. It was almost a shudder. "That may be," he admitted, "but forgive me if I don't feel like thanking you."

Pausing to form his thoughts carefully, realizing they had a whole new segment of a society to which they could extend diplomacy, even friendship, Riker hesitated for a few seconds.

"Hugh," he said finally, "I'm not asking you to be our friend, but maybe we can help each other. Starfleet ships should be heading this way in a couple of days, and we still have some crew on the planet. Help us rescue the captain and his team, and we'll help you fight Lore."

Hugh shook his head abruptly. "It's a bad bargain, Commander. Lore's gunships will destroy your vessels, and a handful of your crew will be no match for the Borg."

"What's the alternative?" Riker pressed. "To sit here in a cave and hope others will defect and join you?"

"Others *will* join us. Many are disenchanted with Lore, but they're afraid to speak out."

Riker bit his lip and kept himself from rattling off the episodes through history when one small band of ragtag fighters had beaten back an impossible tide. He didn't have time to sing all the rebel songs or tell Hugh all the tales of valor that every human child got to hear. Hugh plainly understood that there *was* a future for the Borg as individuals; he just didn't have a clue as to how to get there.

Riker realized there was nothing else he could say. "We came here to get our people. I don't want to cause you any more trouble. . . ."

He gestured at Worf, and the two turned to leave.

From behind him, Hugh's voice came. "Tell me . . . about my friend."

Riker turned to look at Hugh. "Friend?" he said.

"The human called Geordi."

"I wish I could tell you," Riker said. "We think he's being held inside the compound."

Hugh's expression changed to one of concern. He glanced around the cavern at the Borg who were hiding. "I cannot help you," he said uncertainly. "I cannot risk our being discovered."

"Okay," Riker offered. "Don't help us. But will you at least show us how you get in and out of that compound?"

Chapter Fifteen

The Cell

JEAN-LUC PICARD cast a glance at the Borg guard outside the forcefield, then moved to the back of the cell and pretended to fall asleep on the bench. He gestured to Troi.

She nodded.

He turned his head away and listened.

She was moving toward the forcefield.

"May I ask you something?"

Her voice was quiet, unintimidating. Picard listened to it, and hoped the Borg guard was listening too.

"What happened to the people who lived on this planet?" Troi went on, apparently realizing that she had to provide specifics in order to get specifics in return.

"They were biological life-forms," the guard buzzed back, his voice rattling with that robotic Borg sound. "They were weak and imperfect. The One ordered us to destroy them."

Picard listened, his hands and legs tense as he lay there and hoped Troi would pursue the conversation. He stared at the gray wall.

"Do you know where the One came from?" Troi asked.

Another pause. The guard didn't have an answer.

"Think about it," Troi pushed on. "The One wasn't born like you and me. Someone constructed him."

"His builder must have been very wise."

"His builder," Troi parried, "was a biological life-form."

Instantly the Borg responded. "That is not possible."

"Why do you think he was made to look human?" Troi said, going on to the next logical step.

Picard held back a desire to applaud her persistence. All he could do was stay out of the way and make sure the Borg guard felt confident enough to converse with her.

The Borg guard was silent. Did that mean he was disturbed?

Picard gave in to his drumming curiosity and turned just enough to see what was happening.

The guard was almost facing the cell, but was staring past the entrance, obviously deep in thought.

"He was created by an imperfect organism," Troi continued, remaining elegantly cool. "Therefore he is not perfect."

"He is the One," the Borg said.

"Since he's not perfect," the counselor went on in perfect agreement with herself, "then the Borg don't have to do what he says. Do they?"

She asked it in a manner that required no answer.

But Picard was heartened even without that answer. He was seeing something he had thought was out of reach. In spite of their behavior and appearance, the Borg weren't robots. They never were, even before Hugh brought them individuality and Lore perverted that.

As he watched the guard, Picard saw the quivering doubts, the beautiful dilemma, and the moving desires cluttering the guard's face. Where there was doubt, there was hope. The new Borg thought they were doing the right thing. They wanted to do what was right, wanted to perceive right and execute rightness, and they were seeking now the definition of that.

This was the flicker of life that he could use if he moved wisely. Before him, in the eyes of the confused Borg guard, was glinting the demand for the birthright that all intelligent beings shared. The natural right to accept personal merit where due, to stumble for oneself, to avoid—yes, passionately avoid—becoming static and indistinguishable from one another. The right to have opinions that differed and to wrangle over those differences. Picard knew that he, the prisoner, was witness to a turbulent upheaval and breaking forth of true individual intelligence. In time, every Borg could become a hotspur.

If only that happens soon enough for the Federation and, if possible, for us.

Approaching footsteps shattered Picard's thoughts and shocked the Borg guard back to his sentry duty.

Picard came out from his corner just as Lore appeared outside the field.

"Where is Geordi?" Picard asked, keeping control over the demanding note that wanted out. "What have you done with him?"

Lore ignored him and activated the outer control panel of the forcefield. The field shivered, sizzled, and resituated itself to bisect the cell and separate Picard and Troi.

Damn it, Picard thought. *I should have anticipated that and kept her behind me. Once again I've failed to predict his actions and now—*

"Hello, Deanna."

Troi backed away from Lore, but not more than a step or two. She didn't seem afraid. At least not yet.

Picard watched her face, her large black eyes, her beauty, which was now a curse, and saw her muster the training she had been given by Starfleet and the hardened wisdom she had earned by going through life as a lovely woman.

"How beautiful you are," Lore said, as though he had heard Picard's thoughts.

Feeling violated himself, Picard pushed forward toward the hot invisible field. "Leave her alone."

Lore ignored him. He pressed forward toward Troi. "There's no need to pretend. I've seen the way you look at me. Everyone has."

"You're mistaken, Lore," the counselor said, her voice firm and emotionless.

She backed away again, trying to maintain a certain space between them. Too much would give her fears away. Too little would invite him on.

On the other hand, they all knew that Lore would do what he wanted, no matter how Troi played the ugly game, so there was no avoiding him.

"I don't think I'm mistaken," Lore said, his eerie grin plastered across what might as well have been the familiar face of Data, who for so long had been worthy of their trust. "Don't be afraid. I'm not going to hurt you."

Picard pushed against the forcefield, but it pushed back with skittering burns on his skin and his uniform. It would come into his mouth and down his throat if he got any closer.

"Leave her alone," he said again, more forcefully.

Lore glanced at him. "Jealous, Captain? She's mine now, and there's nothing you can do to stop me."

Anger puckered Troi's ivory face. "No matter what you do to me, I do not belong to you."

Lore spun to face her again, his expression suddenly embittered as he was forced to accept the difference between conquest of the body and conquest of the heart. "You don't seem to realize what a privilege I'm bestowing on you."

"I don't care," Troi said. "You're not sacred to those of us who can think for ourselves."

She was winning, and Lore looked as though he would kill her for that.

He reached for her, and Troi lashed out at his face with both fists.

As Lore blinked away the blows, Troi moved toward the wall. Another smile crossed the android's bright face, but it wasn't much of a smile. "I like that," he said. "How did you know?"

"Liar," Troi countered. "You can't fool me, and you can't have me. I know more about emotion than you do, and I'll always win against you."

Picard wanted to tell her to stop, but she was right. She did know more than Lore did, and maybe more than the captain did, about raw emotions and how to use them—for good or ill. He realized that any member of his crew might face a moment like this, when he couldn't help them, but for him to be witness to it . . . He wanted to put his hand through this damnable field and peel the artificial skin off that creature.

Lore glared at Deanna. Then he turned to the cell opening and looked at the Borg guard, who was watching like a curious child who knew that *something* was going on, but didn't know exactly *what*.

And since the Borg were linked in their minds, what this Borg saw, they all saw.

Picard pressed the field again. "You don't want

them to see what you'll have to do to get her," he said, "do you, Lore?"

Lore's expression went cold with bitterness. He wanted to remain perfect in the minds of his followers.

"There will be a better time," he said. "You're very bright, Captain Picard, you know that? Basic, but bright." He swung to Troi and pinched her chin appreciatively. "I'll be back, you can be sure. I'll have you all to myself when the time is right."

Mustering his pride and a posture that would work, he spun around like a toy solder and walked out.

When he was gone, the Borg guard maneuvered the forcefield back into place at the entrance, and Picard and Troi could reach each other again.

"Are you all right?" the captain asked her quietly.

"Of course," Troi said, as though she'd been pawed by some lummox in a bar. "Sir, did you notice something about that encounter?"

"Yes, I certainly did. He wasn't sure what to do to keep his deity intact. He hasn't got things quite as well planned out for the long run as he is proclaiming. He has the next few minutes worked out and a vague idea of the future, but it's *very* vague."

"And that means he can be surprised," she added.

With lowered brow and shoulders tensed, Picard turned to the forcefield and gazed down the stark corridor.

"Let's surprise him."

The Caverns

"These caverns have tunnels that run beneath the compound. Some of them are connected to the environmental control system and then to the corridors in the compound."

Hugh's voice still held remnants of the robotic buzz, but only on certain syllables. He was definitely not just Borg anymore, and confused or not, he could never go back.

Will Riker ducked to avoid getting clipped in the forehead by more low-hanging rock, but he kept his thoughts to himself.

"Show us," Worf said as he brought up the rear. "If we can determine the geography of the compound, we can form a plan to rescue our crewmates."

"You will never get them away from Lore," Hugh said. "We are on a hopeless quest."

His voice sagged as he led them through the dim maze of rock.

Riker stepped close to Hugh's side. "Nothing is hopeless until you give up. Of all the things you've learned, how have you missed that? You're the one who has defied Lore better and longer than any of us. Can't you give yourself credit for that?"

"I deserve no credit," the sad cyborg said. "Lore knows we escaped. Sooner or later he will find out about this place. He will come here, and we will all be killed."

"If it's all so hopeless, why don't you just surrender to him?" Riker asked.

Hugh's shoulders were slumped and his gait uncertain as he walked before them, casting a beam of light from a mechanical implement on his right shoulder. "I don't know," he said simply.

"It's a thing we call risk, Hugh," Riker said. "And good old-fashioned defiance. Freedom carries a price. You know about it, even though you don't think you do. It's almost instinctive in living beings, and you're alive, Hugh."

Hugh didn't turn his head. He pressed his lips tight, his jaw moving as though he wanted to speak but couldn't muster the right words. He paced forward, leading the way, his feet heavy, as if he were dragging his awakening conscience.

Riker spoke again. "You know, Hugh, you're wrong about us. We had an opportunity to use you to completely destroy the Borg collective, and you know what? We didn't do it."

Hugh looked up at him.

Riker leaned forward, determined to get his message across.

"The collective attacked the Federation and killed tens of thousands of people before we were lucky enough to stop it. We still haven't finished rebuilding. We had a way to insert in you a complete shutdown of all Borg—one big computer virus. We could've used you to put an end to the Borg threat. What would the collective have done to us, given the same chance?"

"Then why didn't you do it?" Hugh asked, his face crimped in the poor light.

"Because it would've been wrong!"

Riker's heart was pounding. He heard it drumming in his ears. He needed Hugh on their side, but even more, he suddenly wanted to get another message across. If he died trying to wrap all this up, at least he would've managed to deliver this one bit of mail from one civilization to another.

"We were trying to do what was right," he said. "Not just right for us, but just *right*. If you don't see any difference between us and Lore, then you're not looking. It would've been a violation of everything we are as a species, and Captain Picard knew that. He endured a hell of sleepless nights and a good dressing-down from Starfleet because of the decision to let you go, but that's what life is. Decisions! When you became an individual, we sent you back to live an individual life, because that's what *you* wanted. Which society do you want these new Borg to be part of?"

Squinting in the dimness, Riker watched Hugh as the faint light wobbled and played across their faces. "These kinds of choices, Hugh . . . this is what it means to be alive."

Finally he sighed and stepped back. "Hugh, my friend," he said, "I think we believe in you more than you believe in yourself."

Geordi tried to raise his arms for the tenth time, and for the tenth time was reminded of the straps holding him onto some kind of a tilted platform. It wasn't a bed or even a cot; it was some sort of examination platform. He felt like a creature in a story lying on a doctor's table.

Terror kept his breathing so shallow that he was starting to feel faint. He tried to take a deep breath or two, get some oxygen into his brain and some courage into the rest of him, but it was hard to be brave. He was alone, he couldn't see, he couldn't move, and his best friend had been talking about experimentation.

Not a formula for peace of mind.

He tried to sniff for clues—literally—and listen for them, but wearing the VISOR all these years had spoiled him. It worked so much better than simple vision that he didn't pay much attention to his other senses. It had been years since he'd had to walk and move and get along without it.

Why hadn't he taken the time to learn? He had always had so many other things to do, and the *Enterprise* had always been a perfect haven. He tended the ship, the ship protected him in return, and he always had the VISOR to do his seeing for him.

Now it was gone.

Was that a sound? Was somebody out there?

Footsteps? By looking at the floor with his VISOR, he could tell if someone had walked there. He didn't usually bother to listen.

"Data?" he began. "Is somebody there?"

For a moment there was only the bizarre silence and a feeling that he wasn't alone.

Then: "Geordi."

"Captain!" How had Picard gotten away from the Borg? Did it matter? He was here!

"Shh," the captain said. "We're getting out of here."

"Hurry," Geordi gasped. "Data was just here. He went to get something—"

"Too late." Data's voice.

Geordi drew a harsh breath and held it. He'd been fooled. Data's voice-replication ability.

"My brother suggested I try to develop my sense of humor," Data said. "What do you think?"

Horror took Geordi by the innards. Data's talk of experiments was like something out of a gruesome story, but this . . . Data wasn't just doing what needed to be done. He was purposely tormenting his subject and calling it humor.

Geordi tried to pull away as he heard Data approach, but the straps allowed him almost no movement. "I think it needs a little work."

Data was standing beside the platform—Geordi could sense his presence and feel himself start to sweat again.

A whistling sound, very faint . . . something at the side of his head, at his temple, where the VISOR terminal was. He heard the whistle begin, then felt it vibrate into the side of his head.

"What's happening?" he asked, his voice shivering.

"I am neutralizing your pain receptors," Data said bluntly.

Geordi swallowed hard. Data didn't seem to realize that the pain could be taken away, but the fear wasn't going with it. "What are you doing to me?"

He heard the click and bump as Data put down one device and picked up another.

"I am implanting nano-cortenide fibers in your cortex that are designed to learn and mimic your neural firing patterns."

Something was happening. Geordi felt the pressure at the side of his head, as though a dentist were working on a numbed tooth. He knew there was cold-blooded work being done, felt the pushing on the side of his head and a faint sizzling sensation in his skull.

Sweat poured down his face, broke over his jaw, and drained down his neck. His hands were trembling, pulling up against the straps.

"Once they are in place," Data's voice continued, "I will destroy your existing brain cells and see if the artificial neural network is able to take over cognitive functions."

"Data, listen to me!" Geordi gasped, trying to keep his tone level. "Lore is controlling you. He's transmitting some kind of carrier wave that's affecting your positronic matrix."

"If the procedure is successful," Data continued, "your cognitive processing functions will be considerably improved."

Desperate now, Geordi raised his voice. "Don't you care that he's manipulating you?"

"However, there is approximately a seventy percent chance that you will not survive the procedure."

More pressure. More sizzling. Faint movement against his skull—Geordi gritted his teeth. Weakness flooded into his limbs. If he could only see . . . see mutilation coming, maybe death coming . . .

"I don't care much for those odds," he murmured.

A pause, and Data's voice added, "They are cause for concern."

Concern . . . Was there some part of Data that still cared about him?

He searched frantically for a logical way to awaken the lingering devotion he thought he heard. If there was a chance—

"However," Data went on, "since I also have Counselor Troi and Captain Picard, the odds are that the procedure will be successful on at least one of you."

The cold truth hit Geordi square in the face. He'd misunderstood. And there was nothing he could say that would stop Data from drilling neural fibers into the skull of what once had been his closest friend.

Kind Data, dependable Data, decent and ethical Data, who wouldn't have allowed this mutilation and torture to happen in a million years.

If only Data were really here.

Geordi gritted his teeth harder. As if to mock his fading hope and fan his fear, the pressure at the side of his head began again.

Chapter Sixteen

"HELP ME!"

The alarmed voice pierced the corridors of the compound and drove a shock through even the most controlled mind. Along with it came the sound of the forcefield chittering as its energy was disrupted.

The Borg guard turned abruptly, hesitated an instant or two, then stepped toward the cell where his master's prisoners were being held.

Inside the cell, one of the prisoners was sprawled on the ground, senseless. Picard.

"He tried to escape," the female Troi said as she knelt by the unconscious body. "The forcefield put him into neural shock! If he dies, Lore will blame you!"

The guard hesitated again, but this woman's voice had affected him before and he trusted it, or at least the effect it had upon him.

He deactivated the forcefield and entered the cell. He bent to take a closer look.

Senselessness attacked him almost immediately.

He didn't fully realize what happened.

Silvery fluid dripped from his ripped-out tubing as he slumped to the floor.

Picard rolled over and got up, threw down the detached tube he'd finally managed to get a hand on, and immediately examined the disabled guard's prosthetic arm. He fumbled a moment, then managed to disengage the weapon from the arm and hand it to Troi.

The oldest trick in the book, so old that Picard had almost been embarrassed to try it, but it had worked.

It also proved Counselor Troi's hypothesis—that the Borg had had so little time as independent beings that they were still naive about many things. That could explain how Lore was able to control them.

He added this tidbit to his bag of collected details and continued to formulate a mode of behavior. Eventually he would knit all this into a plan with which to deal directly with Lore.

"See if the corridor's empty," he said.

Troi silently slipped beyond the opening of their cell—and stopped short.

"Drop it, or I will break his neck."

As the familiar voice cut through him, Picard stood up quickly. Troi was already coming back into the cell, pressed back by Data, who was holding Geordi's arm with one hand and gripping Geordi's throat with the other hand.

Picard almost shouted when Troi did as she was told. She shouldn't have surrendered her weapon— that was the first rule of action in a situation like this.

But of course, Deanna Troi wasn't trained for situations like this. She'd had a chance to destroy Data, virtually halving the danger to the Federation, with the loss of only one crewman. An astonishing opportunity.

Yet even so, the counselor, trained to cure, couldn't bring herself to kill. She didn't comprehend that they were all expendable. Geordi could have. Even Data could have—Data as he had been before all this. That was part of command training.

From the look of him, Geordi wasn't going to survive much more of what he was going through. Affected by the sight, Troi had acted instinctively, despite Picard's earlier admonitions of the importance of stopping Data.

Nothing to be done about it now. The weapon was forfeited.

Picard gritted his teeth hard and didn't say anything as Troi rejoined him. Together they stood there, helpless, as Data dragged their groggy engineer into the cell and pushed him toward them.

They caught Geordi and took him to one of the benches. He was limp, his skin sallow and clammy. His eyes were open, their gauzy white unseeing irises threaded with redness.

"What have you done to him?" Picard asked.

Data ignored him. "I will be back for him later."

Coldly he turned, and gestured for two Borg who'd appeared in the corridor to remove their comrade. The pair grasped the fallen Borg guard between them and dragged him out of the cell.

Data kicked away the weapon that was lying on the floor. It skittered down the empty corridor.

A moment later the forcefield came back on.

So much for the escape attempt. They hadn't even put ten feet behind them.

Troi bent over the brutalized engineer. "Geordi, are you in pain?"

"No," Geordi murmured. "I'm a little dizzy . . . but that's all."

Picard took him at his word and pushed them back toward business. He opened his palm and showed Troi a small black and silver mechanism. Speaking quietly, he said, "I was able to take part of a transceiver from the guard's interlink system. It uses a form of phased pulse technology."

Geordi struggled to raise his head. "Maybe we can modify it to . . . generate a kedion pulse . . . and reboot Data's ethical program."

"You'll have to talk me through it."

"We might not have time. Data said he'd be back for me soon." Geordi's voice was ragged, but he fought to think clearly. "Let me lay it out for you. First, you'll have to reroute the modulation circuitry to bypass the initializers. . . ."

Picard listened intently and tried to do as he was

told as fast as he could. Geordi might not possess the energy to repeat himself. If they had any real chance of altering the future as laid out by Lore, they certainly wouldn't manage that with faked injuries and blundered escape attempts.

Working intently on so small a device, the captain let time slip by on its own. How long this took wouldn't matter if he didn't pay attention to what he was doing. Fiber after fiber, he changed the little receiver's reason to exist. Crude work, but the mechanism only had to work; it did not have to be elegant. Some things were so fundamental that delicacy wasn't a consideration. All this device had to do was send the right signal in the right general direction.

All he had to do was get the signal correct and not let anyone notice that he had a hobby.

"Dr. Crusher, I'd like to log a protest."

Barnaby's harsh voice said he wasn't being funny. He was red-faced and troubled, and suddenly everyone on the bridge was looking at him as Beverly Crusher faced him.

She couldn't help acting surprised. "You would?"

"Yes, I would."

"Well . . . go ahead."

He shifted on his feet, back and forth, and finally coughed up what he had to say. "You have your orders," he said. "This isn't what the captain wanted. I think there are some details you're not thinking about."

"I *think*," Beverly bristled, "I'm thinking about forty-seven details you're forgetting, Lieutenant."

The eyes of the other bridge crew were like needles jabbing from all around, but Crusher and Barnaby continued to face each other on the aft deck.

"If Captain Picard hadn't put you in command," Barnaby said, "then I'd be in command."

"Is that what this is all about?" Beverly roared.

He waved his hands. "No! I'm not asking for command! That's not what I mean! What I mean is, if he hadn't put you in command personally, then I or any other line officer would be in command, or somebody else who can actually drive the ship. Choosing you was his prerogative, but it was also his whim. He did that on purpose. It wasn't random. It was like a message. He gave you retreat orders, Doctor, and you are not retreating."

She shook her head. "I wish you'd make your point. He gave me the ship and said, 'You make the decisions.' And that's what I'm doing."

She started to turn away, but Barnaby caught her elbow. "Please, listen. Think about this. It's not as if we jump in and out of these conduits every day. What if the emergency beacon doesn't make it? Or what if it just plain malfunctions? We don't depend on those things for life-and-death messages. They're just not reliable enough. What if there are Borg on the other side of the conduit to pick up the message and destroy it? Or what if Starfleet thinks it's some kind of trick and takes a week to decide what to do about it? We're supposed to go through there and add our faces and our words to the message to Starfleet."

The anger had left his face. Obviously, he had only needed it for a minute, to drum up the nerve to challenge her. Now he was just desperate to make her understand.

"The captain gave us orders to retreat for good reason," Barnaby said, "with more than the lives of forty-seven people in mind. He put you in charge because you weren't likely to engage the Borg in combat. You're supposed to bring in line officers with heavy-duty ships to give us all a real chance. If the *Enterprise* is captured or destroyed, you will have given the Borg a hell of a Christmas present."

Beverly stared at him, her face numb, her hands cold. She hadn't thought of any of those things. The captain, she saw now, had clearly thought of all of it.

"Face it, Doctor," Barnaby finished. "The captain didn't put you in charge of the *situation*. He put you in charge of the *retreat*."

Most doctors grow a pretty thick skin. It takes a lot to get one to pass out or even get sick at a concept.

Beverly felt as if she might do both. He was right. She was commanding like a doctor, not like a line officer.

It was her job to save lives. That was what she always did. Always work to save the life. It was never her thought that the best thing to do would be to *let* people die. She had never had to make a choice like that.

How could a person endure having to say, "These live, those die"?

Jean-Luc had put her in command, and now she was turning that decision into a mistake. Barnaby was right. She'd been entrusted to escape with the ship and report to Starfleet. The captain had expected her to be strong enough to do that.

Other than token Academy classes in emergency command, she didn't have the training for this.

Sudden empathy with Jean-Luc—with any captain—almost made her throw up. She wanted jump up and put Barnaby in charge, then run back down to medical and do what she was comfortable with.

They were all looking at her. They were waiting for her to do that.

But Jean-Luc hadn't put her here to be comfortable either. And being captain didn't mean accepting group decisions. Command wasn't done by committee. Even being a temporary captain might mean redefining her own orders as the situation required.

Her hands were sweating. She clenched them.

"I've made my decisions," she said. "I have to take my lumps. Besides, if this is a mistake, I'll be far too dead to answer to a review board." She nodded at Barnaby. "Your objections are noted. I'll keep them in consideration. Return to your post."

High warp was exhilarating. Especially for a doctor who didn't often get a chance to watch it happening.

Beverly found herself drifting away from the task at hand and just staring at the great forward viewscreen as space peeled away before the starship.

Why did there have to be such a poisonous urgency throwing pall over the beauty before her?

Still unable to get the palms of her hands to stop sweating, she turned toward the aft station. Barnaby was beside her now, and they were both leaning over Taitt, who was pulling up a graphic onto a monitor.

"Sensors still can't determine the Borg ship's location. I'm trying to filter out the interference."

"We'll be within transporter range in nineteen seconds," Barnaby said.

Taitt's voice got high with nerves as she said, "I'm starting to get sensor resolution. . . . There's the ship!"

She gestured at the monitor, which now showed the Borg ship's plane of orbit.

Beverly pointed at the opposite side of the planet. "We'll enter orbit here."

Barnaby nodded. "Helm, new course. Heading zero five two mark seven."

The Conn officer sounded skeptical, but said, "Aye, sir."

"Stand by to drop out of warp in . . . eight seconds," Barnaby directed.

"I hope that gives us time," Beverly said.

Barnaby didn't respond to her. "Emergency deceleration in five seconds . . . three . . . two . . ."

"Hang on!" Beverly couldn't help but say.

"One!"

The ship lurched and shrieked around them as thrusters engaged and the impossible speed fell off like a book falling off a table. Half the bridge officers were thrown to the deck. Taitt slid out of her chair and knocked Beverly in the ankles, but Beverly managed to hang on to the console and stay on her feet.

Barnaby grasped the girl's arm to keep her from rolling forward into the supports of the tactical station, but he had to go down on one knee to do it.

Nausea set in at the last second, then dizziness, then a sense of weight as the gravitational systems battled to get control over the sudden change.

Taitt crawled back into her chair.

"We did it!" she gasped. "Standard orbit, sir! The Borg ship is on the planet's far side. They're moving to intercept us!"

Beverly pushed herself up. "Bridge to transporter room. Begin evacuation!"

Barnaby dived for the sensor panels. "The Borg will be in weapons range in . . . thirty-two seconds."

"Get ready to raise shields," Beverly said, and realized she should've said it ten minutes ago.

"We still can't locate Captain Picard's team," Barnaby reported, "and now there's no sign of Commander Riker or Lieutenant Worf."

Holding back a desire to slap something, Beverly snapped, "Crusher to Salazar. Report!"

"We're pulling the last teams off right now," Salazar said, *"but six people are still unaccounted for."*

"Keep trying!"

She knew she was telling him something he was already doing, and she wished she could be down there helping. Was this what it meant to be captain? This feeling of helplessness? Of wanting to run all over the ship and do everything personally, yet be able only to deligate responsibilities even in an emergency?

On the big screen the Borg ship appeared at the crest of the planet.

"Borg ship powering up its weapons array," Barnaby warned, his voice low.

"Come on, chief, it's now or never," Beverly muttered, glaring at the forward screen, determined to choke every last second out of the transporter process.

Barnaby straightened suddenly and pulled his hands back from his console as if to protect them from being burned. "They're firing!"

Chapter Seventeen

"PORT NACELLE'S BEEN HIT!"

The ship rattled and howled in pain, and slid several points to the left before the helm managed to regain control.

Such a sensation—to feel a multi-thousand ton vessel shake underfoot—the floor that had a moment ago been so secure—

Beverly grabbed for balance and wished she could be anywhere else. "Helm, get us out of here!"

"We've lost warp engines," Barnaby countered.

"Evasive maneuvers!" she shouted back. "Full impulse."

On the forward screen, the planet dropped away

suddenly and was left behind. Even impulse speed was a fast way to enact a sudden turn.

"Shields are down to eighty percent," Taitt reported. All the color was gone from her face except for two scared blue eyes.

"Fire phasers," Beverly said, trying to sound in control. If she could keep her voice steady, the ship and the crew would do what needed to be done. All they needed was her permission to do it.

The ship responded with such swiftness that she almost repeated herself, as though she'd missed something, but a second later Barnaby said, "Direct hit. No damage to the Borg ship."

No damage. No damage? How was that possible?

A bolt struck the *Enterprise,* and the ship buckled around them.

"Shields at thirty percent," Taitt said.

Beverly twisted around, not sure who was monitoring this or that. "Status of the warp engines?"

"Still down," Barnaby said. He glared at the Borg ship. "We can't outrun them."

The acting captain stared too. Aggravation gnawed at her. Her noble plan to rescue the few and sacrifice the many—a thousand people aboard the ship, millions in the Federation, and she'd acted on the most basic of all reflexes—to make herself feel good. Be a heroine. Go back after the forty-seven, most of whom were busy doing their duty better than she was doing hers. They were banding together, pulling out their Starfleet bags of survival tricks, battening down until a dozen starships came to pound through the Borg front and rescue them.

But the starships might not be coming, thanks to her. The only starship within a hundred thousand light-years was streaking off in the wrong direction, with a Borg ship on its heels.

Frustration held her down as if she wore handcuffs. She had neglected the risk involved with her own nobility. She was too much doctor for this job.

Can't outrun them, can't slap them down . . . There must be something they can't take. There has to be something I'm not thinking of, something with more power than the Borg, something . . .

"Helm," she said, not entirely sure of what she was doing, "set a new course." She stopped to think of the piloting details—hoped her pause wasn't long enough to lose the confidence of the people who were watching her, what little they had left. "Heading three four four mark six. Full impulse."

The anxious eyes of her bridge crew all struck her at once.

Well, there went the confidence.

"Sir," Taitt struggled, "that heading will take us directly into the sun."

The Cell

Geordi was gone, taken by two Borg sent by Data.

Interesting, and bothersome, that Data hadn't come back personally to take him away.

That detail nagged at Picard as he worked on the device he had taken from the Borg guard.

He had turned his back on the cell opening, and Troi was standing there to block what he was doing from anyone who might appear there.

Picard felt consummately alone in his purpose. And he was only partially certain of what he was doing. The technology looked familiar, but the arrangements were alien.

"I've done everything Geordi said," he told Troi. "Now we just have to activate the device."

"How are we going to know if it works?" she asked.

"The signal will carry for a radius of seven hundred meters, which will cover the entire compound. So the pulse will reach Data. Whether it will reboot his ethical program . . . we'll only be able to tell by his behavior."

She turned. "Won't he realize something is happening to him?"

"I doubt it," he said. "It's one program among thousands, and it operates in the background of his processors."

The whole concept sounded so simple that Picard couldn't help wondering if he was missing something. An element in the rock . . . something.

He came to the entrance of the cell and glanced down the corridor, then set the transceiver on the floor and nudged it with his toe toward the forcefield.

The little mechanism jumped, caught the forcefield's haze, and sucked at the glow of power.

"I just hope," he said, "that this forcefield has enough energy to trigger the kedion pulse."

The *Enterprise*

"The data banks should contain information about a process called metaphasic shielding."

Beverly hoped she sounded as if she knew what she was talking about, but there was a lingering roughness of doubt in her throat.

"I know about that research," Barnaby said. "Commander La Forge developed a program to implement the shielding—"

"I know. He told me about it," she said. She hoped they would have confidence in this crazy idea if they knew it was Geordi's. Or maybe she was really hoping to share the blame, but at least she had drummed up *something* for them to do about this situation.

The Borg ship was large on the screens and getting larger. All around, the bridge crew worked frantically to pull up Geordi's research on metaphasing and feed it into the right computers.

"Activate the program," Beverly told them. "We'll be able to enter the sun's corona, and the Borg ship won't be able to follow."

Barnaby leaned into his task, his face drawn tight. "But those shields have never been tested. There's no way to know if they'll hold."

"Then we'll test them," she said.

"Sir," Taitt interrupted. "Hull temperature is rising. Now at twelve-thousand degrees centigrade. Radiation level nearing ten thousand rads."

The frenzy had left her voice. Now there was just a calm sense of doom, and with it an acceptance of the fact that they might as well do all they could, because otherwise they were finished. Better to fly into the sun than let the Borg take them and claim a victory.

The Borg weapons flashed. The ship jolted and took a harsh turn, then whined to recover itself.

"Report!" Beverly said.

"No structural damage," Taitt reported hoarsely. "Shields at sixty-eight percent—"

"Lieutenant, activate the metaphasic program. We don't have a choice."

"Aye, sir," Barnaby said grimly.

True, they'd backed themselves up to a point where they had no choice, and now the crazy idea would have to work or they were toast.

Anger roared up in Beverly's chest. Yes, it was better to be toast than to be taken by the Borg. She'd disobeyed her standing orders and given forty-one more people a chance to live, and maybe she was about to throw it all away, but at least she'd done more than behave like a Borg and do as she was told. At least she'd have that to hold to her heart as the ship cracked open around her in the solar inferno.

"Hull temperature is critical!" Taitt said. "We can't withstand this heat much long—"

Barnaby interrupted her. "Okay, I've got it. Engaging metaphasic shield."

It was hard to breathe. The ship was sacrificing systems to fighting the heat. They could feel her trying. A few more seconds and all this would be over. . . .

"Hull temperature dropping," Taitt began, her eyes fixed on the readings. "Down to seven thousand degrees!" She was almost whispering, but the victory in her voice carried across the bridge.

Beverly turned to the helm, holding that victory tight against her chest and glaring at the butcher on the screen, now just a blob in the haze of the sun's corona.

"Maintain course," she said.

"The Borg ship has broken off pursuit," Barnaby reported.

"All stop."

Taitt twisted around. "Sir, the Borg ship is taking up position relative to ours. They're going to wait for us to come out."

Beverly cast her gaze to the viewscreen and the white-light glow of the sun's corona cooking them even as it shielded them. Finally they had found one thing they could take that the Borg couldn't. Even to buy themselves a few extra minutes to think.

"The question is," she tartly murmured, "how long can we stay in here?"

"The last fiber is in place. You have been a most cooperative subject."

Who was that? Someone talking?

"Geordi? Can you hear me?"

"Data? Is that you?"

"Yes."

There should have been fear. But there wasn't.

Geordi lay back again on the tilted platform, its cold surface pressing his shoulder blades, his hips, and stealing all the warmth from his body.

"You know, Data, I've been thinking . . ."

He felt the pressure again on his head, pushing into his skull, picking at nerve endings inside his head. He heard the hum of a medical device scanning him. Any minute, his brain would shut off or be fried by what was happening to him.

Talking helped. His friend had to be in there somewhere, buried under the programming and the outside controls. Data was in there; Geordi believed that, clung to it. He had never been able to accept that Data was all machine. He wasn't. Couldn't be. That would be like trying to be friends with a turbolift, and Geordi couldn't do that. Others looked at Data and saw an android, designed and constructed, but there was more. There were glows of activity that machinery couldn't account for and that Geordi had never been able to track down with instruments. There was benevolence that no machine could manage and a fraternal consideration that a turbolift just couldn't claim.

You're in there, Data. I know you are. If I can just reach you, if the reboot works and I can tap it, then I'll find you. The Data I knew before your so-called

brother took you over. There was life before Lore. . . .
I'll make you remember.

"I was thinking about some of the times we've had together," he said aloud. "Like that time we went sailing on Devala Lake, remember that?"

"I have a complete memory record of that day," Data admitted.

Geordi felt himself smile. "You decided to take a swim . . . but when you jumped out of the boat, you sank straight to the bottom!"

Data's voice beside his ear was too clinical to offer any comfort. "I did not have enough buoyancy to get back to the surface."

Geordi laughed, couldn't help it. He clung to the memories. Just the idea that Data wouldn't have calculated his own buoyancy relative to water before jumping in . . . That's right! This was one of those little things that couldn't be explained if Data was nothing but programming. One of those little anomalies.

"So you had to walk over a kilometer along the bottom of the lake to get back to the shore," Geordi chuckled. He still had an imagination, at least, because he could almost envision the whole thing.

"One kilometer," Data said, "and forty-six meters."

Warmly Geordi added, "It took two weeks to get the water out of your servos."

He felt more pressure, in a different spot. Neural fibers being fed into his scalp. Awful . . .

"It's strange, Data," he said, hoping to distract

himself. "You're able to feel anger, hatred, even a kind of pleasure that comes from being cruel. But humor . . . compassion . . . they elude you. Why?"

"I am still evolving."

The answer came a little too quickly. Geordi hesitated. "But why would you develop the negative emotions first? It doesn't make any sense. Maybe . . . it's because Lore doesn't *want* you to feel good emotions. He knows you would never go along with his plans if you could. I know you wouldn't—"

"My brother wants only what is best for me."

Geordi pushed up against his straps. "He's using a carrier pulse to dole emotions out to you like a drug." Exhausted, he slumped back again. "He only gives you the emotions that suit his needs. And he withholds the rest to keep you under his control. Look, don't take my word for it. Run a self-diagnostic. Don't you owe it to yourself to find out the truth?"

"I am ready to irradiate your existing brain cells."

Data's jarring announcement cracked the reverie, the theories, the efforts. Geordi felt his chances crack, too. Even if the captain and the counselor had managed to build the reboot mechanism and get it activated, it wasn't working. Suddenly he was back on the examining table, being vivisected by a controlled entity.

And the horrors came rolling back.

"Data," he said, "if you ever go back to being the way you were, you may not be able to forgive yourself for what you're about to do to me."

The different tack didn't offer much hope, but Geordi took his last-ditch chance.

Silence pounded between them. Data wasn't answering.

An hour ago Geordi might have found some hope in that silence, but now it offered him nothing. He had so little hope left. He had sweated it all out.

Finally Data's voice made him flinch.

"I am getting some anomalous readings from your neural net. I will have to do further tests before I proceed."

There was a shuffle of movement at his side. Geordi tilted his head and tried to hear, to sense something that would counter the dread he couldn't shake. He wished he could reach out.

"Someone will come," Data said, "and take you back to your cell."

"We can use the environmental control ducts to get inside the compound. They should take us to the cell where the captain is being held."

Worf's voice was serious, heavy, dark, and booming beneath the low ceiling of the caverns.

Riker decided it wouldn't be smart to make any snide comments, like how lucky they were that the compound happened to have air vents big enough to crawl through. Worf probably wasn't in the mood for a joke.

On the other hand, neither am I.

"We'll have to move fast after we stun the guard,"

he said. "The other Borg will know right away that he's been hurt."

"When they realize we are here," Hugh agreed, "your escape route may be compromised."

"We'll have to take that chance."

Riker turned and peered through the cavern.

Hugh gazed back at him. His life-support tubes pulsed like heartbeats, quick and nervous, betraying his lingering doubts, but also showing how deep Riker had managed to dig under the resentment.

The reluctant leader of disenfranchised Borg looked suddenly young, like a teenager trying to decide which bundle of nerves to respond to. If he knew how to help them any more than he had so far, he was still unable to take that step.

At Riker's silent request, Hugh's worried eyes seemed to retreat into the pasty gray complexion.

He parted his lips. "Good luck, Commander."

The landscape outside the compound was broad and changeable. To the left, forestlands. To the right, scrubby rocks and brush. There was the sound of birds and insect life rousing under the sunlight.

A breathable atmosphere—a rarity in the expanse of the universe. Data scanned the area and instantly analyzed it. Trees similar to Earth's boxwoods, wild tangerine, ivy vines, wild hops, cork oak, various species of pine, some wood fern, some puffball fungi, toadstools, and patches of moss and weeds.

There was a body of water out there somewhere, but he could not pinpoint it.

The scents of growth and life flooded his olfactory sensors, triggering memories.

In the near distance, groups of Borg moved about, working at some task put to them by the One. Possibly experiments. Tests.

Data chose not to speculate. Lore would tell him what he needed to know.

He approached his counterpart, who lingered at the compound opening, where he could survey the activities out there.

"Look at them, brother. It's all so simple." Lore waved a hand across the landscape, taking in his world and his workers. "Enemy ships may soon ply the heavens, yet they go on as if nothing threatened them, because they know I will protect them. I tell you, brother, the burdens of leadership are greater than you can imagine."

"I do not generally imagine," Data told him. "I find the results inaccurate."

Lore tightened an arm around Data's shoulders. "I'm so glad you're here to help me. You're the only one I can really trust. We're family. Nothing can compare with that bond."

Imperceptibly, Data gave in to an urge to pull away and put a space between himself and Lore. "I recently ran a self-diagnostic," he announced, "and I discovered that my positronic net is being affected by incoming emissions."

Lore paused. His salesmanlike smile fell away. "Why did you run a self-diagnostic? Don't you trust me?"

"It is my habit to run periodic checks on all my systems. You should do the same."

He was telling the truth. It was in his programming to speak accurately and not to deceive.

Leaving out facts was not the same as lying, however.

He heard echoes of his life among humans, where these lines were not so clearly drawn—yes, he remembered everything, just as he had told the others. Memories placed before him in moving pictures, with no sensation, no satisfaction.

There *had* been sensation and satisfaction the first time through those myriad events, those exchanges of personality with living beings.

Why did he retain only part of the memories now? Only the static images?

Lore regarded him with a narrowed gaze. "I wasn't going to tell you, because I thought it would be better for you to feel as if you were doing it all yourself. The pulse is designed to speed your emotional development by initiating cascade fluctuations in your net. I want to help you, little brother, any way I can. Have you made any progress with La Forge?"

Data frowned, felt his face contort with a small effort. He wanted to continue discussing his changes, these feelings he was experiencing, but now was compelled to change the subject.

He didn't want to change it. He wanted to clarify his role in all this, and Lore's role in his changes.

Lore's gaze was irresistible.

"It is too early to tell if the nano-cortical fibers have performed their function," Data replied.

"I suspect none of the humans will survive the process." Lore sighed with artfully casual regret in his tone. "But it's their own fault, isn't it? They should never have come here." He shook his head and turned once again to survey his landscape and his subjects. "What were they thinking?"

Data heard his brother speak, that voice with so many tonal changes—his own voice, but with many levels he had not yet mastered. Lore's voice sounded like his own voice.

But human.

What were they thinking?

"They came looking for me," Data said, staring out over the landscape.

Lore glanced at him. "Humans are so sentimental."

A simple answer.

Powerful apprehensions drove Data to turn his gaze now to the sky. "I betrayed them. If they die . . . I am responsible."

Suddenly turning to face him directly, Lore studied his face in a fashion that made Data wish to back away. "Why are you talking like this? Is something wrong with your programming? Perhaps I should check your systems."

"I do not want you to check my systems," Data told him with abrupt clarity. "I must resolve these issues myself."

Lore circled him warily. "I think I've made a mistake. I don't believe you can tolerate the amount of emotion you've been experiencing."

Data leaned away but could not mobilize himself to leave the area.

Bringing his hands up, Lore flipped up one of his own fingernails. The circuitry underneath blinked silently.

Such circuitry was commonplace for Data and had never seemed threatening, but just as some humans were sickened by the sight of blood, today he felt revolted by what he was seeing.

"Perhaps I should cut back a little." Lore tampered with the circuitry.

A blistering sensation ran through Data's head, down his neck, through his shoulders, and into his limbs. A moment ago he wanted to move and did not. Now he could not. Emptiness pulled at him. The draining of lubricant . . . loss of power . . .

"How's that?" Lore asked.

Data parted his lips and found them dry. "I . . . do not like it . . ."

"Ah." His brother nodded. "Then you prefer having more emotions?"

"Yes . . ."

"They give you pleasure."

"Yes, please . . . I want more."

He was cold. Blank. The emptiness expanded, weakening his limbs, fogging his memory banks. He yearned for more . . . for anything.

"All right," Lore said. "For now, a little more."

Again he tampered with the circuitry in his finger.

Floods of emotion pushed at Data as though the planet's gravity had suddenly increased. Glowering thoughts flashed in his mind without organization.

He battled to organize them, but the flood was powerful and cold. Surges of the anger he had sought and failed to find, and here it was, gushing into him at Lore's bidding.

Anger. Envy. Savage brutality. Soreness of the mind. These boiled at him in waves. Temper twisted his inner circuits. He felt excitable and wanted to be dared. He wanted to go somewhere and make someone dare him.

"Thank you," he rasped, and he turned away to go look for something to hate.

"Don't mention it," Lore called as his counterpart disappeared back into the compound. "I just hope this has helped clarify things for you."

He waited until he could no longer hear Data's telltale footsteps on the stone floor of the corridors. Then he beckoned to Crosis.

As the Borg stooge approached, Lore shook his head and continued to peer into the corridors.

"I am concerned about my brother," he said. "Crosis, I don't believe he really wants to be part of our great future."

Chapter Eighteen

TROPICAL HEAT burned right through the imaging relays of the forward viewer. Even with the compensators working until they smoked and the screen automatically shading what was out there, the sheer power of a sun at proximity range couldn't be dampened. The brightness moved and surged with every volcanic heave in the sun's corona.

Hiding here in this very hot haven, the *Enterprise* was a very hot boat.

Beverly thought she'd pass out if they had to stay here much longer.

"Hull temperature's rising," somebody reported from the starboard side.

Beside her at the aft station, Barnaby offered yet

another of his many grim truths. "Sir, metaphasic shielding is losing integrity."

No surprise. Nothing—no trick, science, or sorcery—could allow them to stay here for very long. It was a miracle they'd stayed here this long.

"Can you stabilize it?" she felt obliged to ask.

"No," he said flatly. "We won't be able to stay in here more than another three or four minutes."

"Do we have warp engines yet?"

"The last estimate was another half hour."

Grim silence fell. No options.

"Sir?" Taitt interrupted. "I have an idea. . . ."

Beverly stepped toward her and shot her an expression that said "Talk."

No, actually, it said *"Talk!"*

"I think," Taitt said, "we could induce a solar fusion eruption that would destroy the Borg ship."

Barnaby almost knocked Beverly aside. "What?"

Nervous, Taitt turned in her chair. "We'd need to direct a highly energetic particle beam onto the sun's surface. It *should* disrupt the photosphere and produce a superfluid gas eruption. If we target the right spot, the eruption could envelop the Borg ship."

Barnaby's mouth dropped open. He stared at her and shook his head, then shook it again.

Beverly watched his reaction and tried to judge it. A crazy idea was worth pursuing under these circumstances, but it was also just plain sensible to watch the reaction of the most qualified person on the bridge.

She swung to Taitt. "How do you know this'll work?"

As soon as the words jumped from her lips, she heard how stupid a question that was. If it didn't work, so what? Given the circumstances, they were already doomed, so they might as well act crazy.

After all, they had a whole sun at their fingertips, and even the Borg weren't as powerful as a torrid, fuming, blistering solar firebox.

"I did my senior honors thesis on solar dynamics," Taitt was saying. "I hypothesized that it could work."

Beverly just stared at her and blinked the sweat out of her eyes to drain down her temples.

"Excuse me," Barnaby said, "but this isn't the Academy. And a student's thesis is a long way from a workable plan."

Taitt leaned forward to direct a glare at him. "I've already configured the tractor emitters to create the particle beam, and I've targeted a point on the surface so the eruption will engulf the Borg ship."

Her tone said what Beverly had been thinking. Why not? What did they have to lose?

"If her calculations are off," Barnaby pressed, "the eruption could engulf *us.*"

Taitt eyed him. "Well, I'll just have to make sure my calculations are accurate."

There was a definite combativeness in her voice now that she'd been goaded by the cloying heat and the knowledge that they had to try something or go out and face that Borg ship without warp power to back them up. She could afford to be blunt now. She might as well.

Beverly straightened her back. "Let's do it."

"Yes, sir!" Taitt replied.

Apparently Barnaby caught the streak of desperate hope. He plunged for his controls and picked up on what Taitt was doing, enhancing anything she had trouble finding, focusing anything she had trouble focusing upon, plotting distances, measuring solar reactions, gathering the sun's power to do their bidding once—just *once*.

They all knew how tough the Borg ships were. Fire at them, do no damage; be fired upon and lose half your power. Borg ships had attacked the Federation and nearly won, against starship after starship. . . .

"Come on, come on," Beverly murmured, staring at the hazy shape of the Borg ship beyond the sun's blast-lamp brightness on their screens.

"Working," Taitt squeaked, but her voice caught in her throat. She was betting not only her career but her life as well. All their lives.

"Calculations complete," Barnaby said, "I hope—"

"Fire," Beverly told him instantly.

"Firing!"

The ship shivered with added effort as energy was stolen from the precious metaphasing and funneled into a beam that pierced the sun's corona and drilled to its surface, thin as a wagon master's whip.

Almost instantly the sun bucked in reaction. The great natural blast furnace kicked outward with an arm of superheated corrosive power. The eruption caught the Borg ship in a giant thermocautery and turned it into so much scoria in a half second.

Faster than phaser fire. Faster than thought.

"She did it!" Barnaby choked. "The Borg ship has been destroyed!"

Shocked at the speed of their trick, Beverly stared at the screen, squinting until her eyes hurt. Was that it? Was it done so quickly?

How many Borg lives were ended now because of her? Rationally she understood how things had to be, but her instincts pulled at her down. Thousands of lives, even Borg lives, had just been snuffed out on her order.

Did captains feel this way? Did they hide their distress or was it trained out of them?

Tears pressed at the back of her eyes. She fought them down. Couldn't let the crew see. She'd already made a sackful of mistakes—weakness would have to wait its turn.

To keep control of her expression, she gritted her teeth hard and held her breath for a pulsebeat.

She suddenly couldn't wait to hand Picard his damned ship again, run back to sickbay, and spend the rest of her life wondering why anyone would want to be in command and be forced to make these decisions every day.

"Helm!" she shouted. "Take us back to the planet! Full impulse!"

Her throat was raw. She felt like the one who had been blowtorched.

But she'd never again let anyone tell her a sun wasn't a living thing.

"The situation is too ugly now. We can no longer hope to maneuver it to our advantage. We can no longer expect to survive. That changes everything. We've gone beyond saving our own lives."

Jean-Luc Picard paced the cell with burgeoning ire. He felt hot. He'd felt that way for a half hour, if he could still rationally judge the passage of time. He couldn't get the parching out of his throat, or the sensation of being caught on a turnspit.

He paced before the forcefield, back and forth until he felt nauseated, letting the active energy lift the hairs on his arms and remind him of the moment's severities.

At the side of the cell, Troi sat on the bench where La Forge lay. Picard saw that his words were affecting Geordi, but it was time. All Starfleet personnel knew they might face this moment when it was their turn to throw themselves on the gun.

La Forge was weak, but paying attention to the captain. His brown face was dusty with fatigue and strain, painted with sweat but resolute.

Troi was enduring despair in funereal silence.

"It now becomes our responsibility," Picard went on, "to stop this cancer here and now, before it advances into Federation territory again. We must stop Lore and Data in any way possible. I want you both to understand that. If there has been any theme to these events, we must comprehend that it has been a good thing, not a bad one, that the three of us have been captured."

He stopped pacing and turned to face them, determined that they shouldn't miss his meaning. He should have explained all of this to them hours ago.

Troi was watching him, her eyes dark with grief. La Forge's face was turned toward him, and he was listening.

"We might easily have wandered the surface of this planet for days and never discovered Lore's plot," Picard went on. "Once the *Enterprise* set off for Federation space to rouse Starfleet on our behalf, we could have become lost in those valleys and been useless to our fellow soldiers against this cause. But that's not what happened. Now, though we will very probably die, we will die with our goal clear and with a chance to succeed. We have a chance that other people look back in history and wish someone had possessed—a chance to prevent a holocaust before it begins."

He drew a deep breath, squeezed his fists tight, and forced himself to stand very still.

"Our purpose now is to stop Data and Lore at any cost. Ultimately we will be separated, and those are your standing orders."

The cell held his words for a heartbeat, then fell heavily silent.

"Aye, sir," La Forge responded. He sounded much too ready to fulfill that order, as though the words were finally a relief for him.

Troi fixed her eyes on the wall beyond the engineer's shoulder. "Yes, Captain."

"Very well," Picard droned. "They're keeping us in this cell for a reason. Eventually they'll take us out of it. When that happens—"

The forcefield behind him suddenly intensified, then snapped away.

He pivoted and stepped back just before Data appeared at the cell entrance pointing a weapon.

Sudden desire to physically attack the android shot through the captain, just before the pitiful reality hit him: Data could lift all three of them with one hand and throw them against the wall.

Picard moved between Data and the other two. This time he felt something in his own posture that hadn't been there before, as though his own words had fallen most heavily upon himself. He had failed until now to be the center of events. No more.

"You're killing Geordi," he said. "He won't survive another session."

Data stopped walking forward and glared at him.

Perhaps he saw in Picard what Picard had found in himself—the courage to be the one to die first and most horribly on behalf of his crew. If anyone was to be taken this time, it would be Picard.

He didn't quite expect to have his wish granted so easily, but Data waved the weapon and said, "I did not come for him. I came for you."

Relief washed through the captain's mind. Whatever happened now, at least he would be at the core of it and possibly be a catalyst in bringing it all to a swift, if not peaceful, end.

He glanced back at Troi and La Forge.

The young engineer was sitting up partially, against the stone cell wall, the nano-cortical fibers protruding from his scalp, each fiber catching a beam of the artificial light from the corridor. There was fear in his face for what Picard was about to endure.

Troi swallowed a few times but said nothing.

Picard told them with his glance that their new mission was about to begin and that he would be the one to initiate it.

Follow your orders, he urged them with his eyes, *and we will change the future.*

She nodded.

Message received, obviously. They would both think about it while he was gone, and the necessary courage would rise.

Without looking back, Picard strode through the cell and let Data reactivate the forcefield. There was a certain elemental victory in striding forward as though he knew where they were going.

"Do you remember your Starfleet oath, Data?" he asked, keeping his eyes forward.

"Yes, of course," Data said.

"You're breaching it left, right, and backwards, do you know that?"

Telltale hesitation broke the android's stride. "Yes," Data finally admitted.

"You've perpetrated a dozen acts that are grounds

for court-martial," Picard said smoothly. "However, I understand that you have been under the control of an extraneous force. I'm willing to take that into consideration."

"Fine."

A quick answer, in an annoyed voice.

So there was more than just mechanics at work. There were emotions.

Picard had always suspected that Data was quite capable of emotion, more so perhaps than Data himself realized, without interference from Lore, without the ethical programming or tampering from outside. Any being capable of independent thought would eventually be affected by those thoughts, capable of defining and acting upon complex concepts of right and wrong and all the subjective abstracts in between.

Picard knew his crew sensed all this in Data, or they could never have worked with him so closely for so long.

We know you're in there somewhere, Data, deeper than any program can explain. You always have been.

"It's not too late," Picard ventured as Data led him into the main Borg hall. "If you remove the fibers, Geordi might recover."

"That will not be possible," Data said as he gestured farther into the hall.

"Why? Because Lore says so?"

"It is for the greater good."

"Good and bad, right and wrong," Picard said. "Those are functions of your ethical program."

"That is correct."

The captain stopped and faced him down. "What does your program tell you about what you're doing to Geordi? About what you and Lore are doing to the Borg?"

Data didn't react overtly. He did stop advancing though, and the weapon in his hand wavered. His yellow eyes narrowed as he grappled with the questions.

"It tells you these things are wrong, doesn't it, Data? How can actions that are wrong lead to a greater good?"

Data stepped back, briefly unsteady. "You are attempting to confuse me."

"No, Data, you're not confused. You're sensing the truth. Your ethical program is fighting the destructive emotions Lore is giving you."

Anguish crumpled Data's face under a burden of effort. The weapon slipped another inch toward the floor.

One more inch—

"There you are, Captain."

Data's voice—no, it was Lore's—trampled over the progress Picard had been making.

Lore strode into the hall, leading a clutch of his Borg followers. "Thank you for joining us," Lore said. "You're going to help me in a most important ceremony."

Crosis and the other Borg gathered along the periphery of the hall and took up positions that allowed them to watch in silence whatever they were about to be taught.

Lore faced Data squarely and raised his voice.

"It's time to put your doubts aside, brother. It's time to close the door on your past and commit yourself to the great work that lies ahead of us. I need to know that I can count on you."

He turned again and waved his hand.

"As proof," he said, "I want you to kill Captain Picard."

Chapter Nineteen

"I DON'T THINK we'll ever see the captain again."

Geordi's words fell hard on Deanna Troi as she tried to keep him from sweating away all the fluids in his body.

There wasn't much she could do but try to keep him still.

She knew he was anxious to jump up and make good on the captain's last orders—to die as well as they could and to take Data and Lore with them in the name of the Federation.

"Things may change," she told him.

"You're dreaming," he said. "You didn't feel the change in Data. I did. He was ready to do anything Lore told him to do. It just wasn't my friend Data. If

I had to kill the creature calling himself Data today . . . I think I could."

"I'm sorry you feel that way, Geordi. That doesn't sound like you."

"It didn't sound much like Data either, Deanna," he said. "You heard the captain. He's right. We have a job to do. We all know what it is; we just don't have to face it very often. Well, now we've gotta face it."

She shook her head and frowned. "I've never heard you speak this way."

"I'm a Starfleet officer, Deanna," he said. "Never mind the fact that I spend most of my time playing with circuits and conduits. Look at what he did to me. . . . I don't want this to happen to anybody else. I sure don't want it to happen to you. I'm willing to do what I have to, just as Captain Picard said."

Deanna sighed heavily. "Oh, Geordi . . ."

She had no idea what to say to him, and she sensed every surge of noble determination inspired in him by the captain's words, as well as the dismay he was beating down and the plaguing comprehension that the captain had been right—that it was time to kill.

She thought she might be about to die when her sensations were drowned in a blasting sound and half the corridor fell away outside the cell opening.

The two of them threw up their hands instinctively as bits of rock struck the forcefield and ignited a lather of sparks.

Deanna jumped to her feet, but didn't have time to take so much as a single step before the sound of running boots hammered the corridor. There was nothing for her to use as a weapon, not even a stone to throw—

Will! And Worf! Outside the cell!

She rushed to the forcefield, so close that it picked up strands of her long black curls.

"Where is the captain?" Worf demanded unceremoniously as he worked at the panel outside to deactivate the forcefield.

"Data took him away," she said as the field dropped.

Will Riker rushed to her side, an electrical current of relief and concern running hot between them, and at the last moment he gestured at Geordi, who was struggling to sit up.

"There's not much time. Can Geordi walk?"

"He'll need help," Deanna said. She grasped Geordi's arm, and Will caught him on the other side.

"There's an air duct in the corridor that connects to the tunnel underneath the compound," he instructed. "You take Geordi through that duct, and we'll look for the captain."

She nodded, connected with him in a fundamental gaze, and saw in his face that he read her perfectly.

And she knew her eyes told him, *Hurry!*

Chapter Twenty

The Borg Hall

PICARD STOOD before Data and assumed his most implacable posture. He held his eyes unmoving, his shoulders back, arms down.

If Data intended to follow the order given to him by this megalomaniac, then that order would be carried out upon his staid commanding officer without so much as a flinch from his victim.

If Data meant to initiate himself fully into the realm of mindless obeisance, then his hazing would be faced down by ultimate individuality.

Fearless, Picard glared at Data as though Lore and the Borg audience were vanishing around them. For these last seconds, Data would answer to him once and finally.

And he wasn't dead yet.

The realization struck him right through his own determination. He certainly should be . . .

Data was staring back, electric bewilderment charging his features. Somehow, between Lore's control and the signals from the ethical program, he was rising to independent thought. He was a child, awakening to rub his eyes and discover the difference between dream and reality and to find that the dream was the colder of the two.

His lips hung open, his decision dangling in the air.

"No," he murmured. "It would be wrong. . . ."

From one side, Crosis snatched the weapon from Data, who glanced down at his empty hand.

Lore shook his head. "I didn't think you'd be able to do it. You've spent too many years among humans."

As if seeing Data had become too painful, Lore turned away.

Picard was watching carefully enough to see the connections between Lore and Crosis, and sure enough, Crosis barked, "Hold him!"

Two Borg lunged forward to snatched Data by the arms.

With a wave to the assembled Borg along the walls, Lore said, "I've asked many sacrifices of you! Sacrifices I knew were necessary to build a better future. I want you to know that I ask no more of you than I am prepared to give myself. I am willing to make the greatest sacrifice of all . . . my own dear brother."

He reached out to another Borg and was handed a weapon for himself.

Playing at a great sadness that no semi-mechanical being could tell from the real thing, Lore turned back to gaze upon Data. Picard saw the pretense for what it was worth, but what was there to do? Appeal to these Borg?

There was a time, he was ashamed to say, when he could understand them. That time was past. These were evolved beings, and he could not deduce in what direction they had developed.

Lore was raising his weapon. Picard tensed his legs—reflex, to save his officer from extermination? Or do as he had ordered Troi and La Forge—let Data be killed?

Instinct flooded through him. He tensed forward. He would show Data one last truly human act—

A black-gray flash invaded his periphery.

Someone shouted, "No!"

Picard ducked out of the way, answering his instincts from another direction.

One of the Borg jumped to the stage and shoved Lore's weapon up, away from Data, so hard that the weapon flew out of Lore's hand and cracked against the stone.

Hugh!

Crosis whirled, his own weapon raised to slaughter Hugh, but another phaser bolt, a good old-fashioned bolt of bright red Starfleet phaser fire, cut across the room. Crosis's face erupted with shock as he was struck in the chest. He went down boiling with the thousand emotions he had once thrown in the faces of those who now broke from their hiding places.

Picard straightened up and quickly spotted Riker and Worf at attack stance deep in the hall, ready to fire again. Around them, Borg loyal to Hugh and to themselves as individuals jumped from the crowd and charged Lore's followers.

Pandemonium broke out. Borg against Borg, hand to hand. Impossible to tell the Robin Hoods from the sheriff's men.

Picard watched the scene almost as if viewing a historical tape, for this *was* history occurring before his eyes.

The Borg were making their own history.

Though he was hungry to participate, even to orchestrate, Picard forced himself to back away and motioned for Riker and Worf to do the same. Phaser fire dropped off as his officers obeyed him, letting Hugh and his people fight their own battle.

Hugh's forces, finally in charge of their own destiny, caught the rhythm, and the heat of the melee intensified. The noise level rose as the Borg shouted and howled at each other, wide-eyed and catching the fire of their purpose. Motioning to his men to stand by, Picard wanted to believe the medieval philosophy that those whose quest was purest would be the ones to succeed, but he'd faced reality all his life and was standing by to tilt at the odds with phasers if necessary.

As the Borg howled and fought around him with newly characteristic viciousness, Picard nodded at

Riker and thought he got a nod back. Riker held his phaser up but ready. Good—he understood.

A flash caught the captain's attention in a field of thrashing motions. Worf was waving at him and pointing toward one of the entrances.

Picard ducked a pair of wrestling Borg and glowered to show that he didn't know what Worf wanted him to look at. An instant later he comprehended that Worf wanted him to see not something, but nothing.

A terrifying nothing.

Data and Lore were both gone.

The Lab

Data knew where to go. Something within him told him where Lore had gone.

He felt the pulling of causes and desires in his mind, pulses from two directions, three, maybe more. He could not identify the sources of all his thoughts, nor did he want to. These were *his* thoughts.

He would rise above the impulses being received. He would not be controlled. Independence was the mark of a living thing.

"Lore!" he called. He gripped his phaser firmly but could not yet make himself raise it.

Lore stood working frantically at a computer console made of cannibalized parts from various conquests, and even from pieces of conquered Borg who had refused to bend to the wishes of the One. Now he turned.

"Be careful with that weapon, brother," he said, his expression suspiciously amiable. "Somebody could get hurt."

"What are you doing?" Data asked him. A direct question. No intimidation intended. He wished to receive a direct answer in response.

"I have a way out of here," Lore said. "I'm willing to forget about what happened back there and take you with me." He smiled and tilted his head conspiratorially. "We don't need anyone else. We're brothers."

Definition: brothers—1. male children who have the same parents or who have one common parent; 2. males who share common allegiance, character traits, or purpose.

Parent? No. He and Lore were products of the same builder, not a parent. Not a nurturer whose values they could ponder and choose from, emulate or discard in an effort to become better.

And there was no common allegiance for them. Lore had offhandly proclaimed them brothers, and Data had accepted that claim.

An error. No—a mistake. Something an intelligent creature might make.

Mistakes could be corrected.

He stood unmoved by Lore's invitation.

Lore lowered his chin and intensified his gaze as he offered a bribe. "I'll give you the chip our father made. It contains more than just emotions. It has *memories* . . . memories our father wanted you to have."

Lore moved his finger, and Data shuddered from deep within himself. The gush of sensation from Lore was suddenly cut off, and Data felt himself being sucked empty.

This time, though, he didn't fight it.

Better to be empty than to be manipulated. He raised his phaser and prepared to aim.

Movement flashed across his sensory inputs. Lore was diving to one side, reaching for a weapon on the console. Lore was twisting toward him now.

Without pausing to analyze either his counterpart's purpose or his own, Data opened fire.

As the bolt of energy lanced from his weapon, Data allowed himself to endure the satisfaction of doing the one thing no machine could do. He made his own choice.

His hand remained tight on the phaser until the weapon had discharged more than enough destructive energy to penetrate Lore's thoracic shielding.

Overload. Lore froze in step, nerves drawing inward, head tilting upward, arms back, legs beginning to shudder. Threads of electrical feedback crackled around his head and shoulders as his systems overloaded.

His face—was this astonishment?

Data released the trigger of his phaser, and the inevitable played itself out from within Lore's body. Disruption. Superreaction. Breakage.

When Lore fell, the floor reverberated with his weight, so excessive for his narrow body.

His body, and Data's.

Brothers . . . but only in appearance.

Data knelt beside the sputtering form. The impact of the fall had broken open the camouflaging flap on the side of Lore's head. Bared circuitry hissed out of order and effervesced with surging power that would soon burn critical connections.

Lore's eyes were open, of course, but there was also focus.

He gazed up at Data, and there was unmistakable sadness there.

Data refused to be moved. "I am going to deactivate you now," he said.

Clearly damaged, Lore tried to gather enough connections to speak.

"If you . . . do that . . . you will never . . . feel emotion again. . . ."

Data put down his phaser and found one of the tools he had used to inflict unthinkable torment upon Geordi.

But he would not think about that. He would complete the task at hand.

He would execute Lore.

"I know," he said, "but you leave me no other choice."

The words were easily spoken, but his inner systems contradicted them. He knew what a choice was now, and he knew he was making one. He could elect to repair Lore, to try to make use of so valuable a commodity, so rare a being, to explore the compli-cated construction that allowed Lore to be what he was, and have the expanse of thought that he had . . . Lore was the key to the next step in his evolution.

But he did have a choice. He was making it.

"Good-bye, Lore," he said.

Lore blinked up at him, but only once or twice. Most of his systems were paralyzed now. "I . . . love you . . . brother."

Of his own accord, with decisions made from his own thoughts, regardless of incoming signals or absent instructions, Data completed the last step in the shutdown.

The little lights stopped blinking. Lore was still. His eyes remained open, but there was no life.

There was no Lore.

The Hall

"Enough!"

Showing that he was certainly a living being, Hugh emerged from the stumbling tangle of cyborg bodies, gasping out his command with enthusiasm. He seemed surprised.

"Enough," he said again, and this time everyone heard him.

Captain Picard motioned again to Riker and Worf to hold back. From where he stood, he could see Riker with his foot on one of Lore's Borg, phaser aimed down into the entity's pasty face, and Worf holding the wrists of another.

All around, dead and injured Borg littered the hall. Hugh's comrades—how could he tell them from any other of their kind?—were holding off the remaining few of Lore's followers, who seemed to have lost their will to resist. Or perhaps they had lost their purpose when they saw their leader retreat.

Not the first time in history.

Hugh's Borg friends seemed confused about what to do next. Hugh stood above them on Lore's platform, looking around, not sure of the next stage in his conquest.

Picard straightened and wished he knew the origin of this conflict. What was Hugh doing here in the first place? Why had he decided to fight?

Riker must know—he and Hugh had appeared at the same time. There had to be a connection.

Letting his curiosity lapse until later, Picard stepped toward the platform. "Hugh," he said, "congratulations on your victory."

Hugh turned to him, blinked, then managed only a nod.

"Captain!" Riker was crossing toward him, holding his phaser in one hand and his communicator in the other.

"It's the *Enterprise,* sir. They're approaching the planet!"

No more welcome words had ever been spoken, but Picard's brow dropped and he roared, "Why are they here? They couldn't possibly have reached Starfleet and come all the way back already. What happened?"

"Dr. Crusher has armed parties standing by," Riker said. Apparently he didn't want to answer Picard's question or accidentally get in the line of this particular fire.

"Give me your communicator," the captain ordered.

Riker reached over a clutter of downed Borg and almost tossed the communicator rather than get too close.

"This is Picard," the captain barked.

"Crusher here, Captain. It's good to hear your voice."

"I'm glad you think so. Your opinion may change when we get the opportunity to discuss this later. There is a Borg vessel guarding this area—"

"The Borg vessel has been neutralized, sir."

He paused, and he and Riker stared at each other.

"Neutralized?" he asked.

"Destroyed, sir. It wasn't easy, but we had the sun on our side."

Picard tried to absorb the fact that this wasn't some kind of joke. "Yet another story I can't wait to hear," he said. "I want you to use your sensors to locate Troi and La Forge. They're somewhere inside the lower levels of this compound—"

"Sir, I've got them both," Riker interrupted. "I can give the ship their coordinates."

Picard paused, gave him a surprised-but-pleased blink or two, then said to Dr. Crusher, "Belay that. Commander Riker will provide you with the numbers. Stand by." He shoved the communicator back. "Do it."

"Aye, sir. *Enterprise,* this is Riker."

The captain stepped over the twitching pile of cyborg bodies and past Riker.

As Worf and the other Borg watched him, he approached Hugh—slowly.

"Thank you," he said. "Your arrival certainly turned the tide for us."

Hugh nodded again, still unsure of what to do with his victory. "I would not have challenged Lore's followers. I wouldn't have thought this could happen for us. But *he* talked to me."

Another nod, this time at the *Enterprise's* first officer, who was still speaking into his communicator, doing his best to clean up what had very nearly been a fatal mess for them all.

Picard's anger mellowed somewhat. His crew did know what to do, and situations were unpredictable.

Hugh was gazing at the dead and dying.

"What is it, Hugh?" Picard prodded.

The cyborg's face became animated with questions. "These once were my own kind," he said, "but I don't recognize them anymore. They still look like me, but in the evolution of a culture, they have become the enemy. This is difficult for me to absorb. We once worked together for a common purpose."

"You had no common purpose," Picard shot back. "You had a common urge to conquer. They're not the same."

He stepped closer and lowered his voice.

"Any colony of ants can work together," he said. "You know that from your former life. But none of you really got anything out of being automatons, did you? The collective moved and grew, but only physically. There was no real advancement, and nothing good came out of it. Intelligent individuals working together—that's the true jewel of freedom. If it were easy, it probably wouldn't be any more worth having than the raw force of the Borg collective. Hugh," he added quietly, "teamwork is not the same as collectivism. There's nothing wrong with choosing between them. In fact, there's great *human* strength in teamwork."

Hugh's brow puckered, but he didn't take his eyes away from Picard. The uncertainty began to slip as he acknowledged the courage he and his followers had just displayed. He was beginning to understand that he wasn't in the collective anymore and that it was the responsibility of an individual to act individually. Being chattel by choice—that would have been the real tragedy.

Picard stepped away briefly, to let the concept simmer. He called to Riker, "What about La Forge and Troi?"

Riker looked up. "The *Enterprise* is in orbit. They're both aboard. I—"

A murmur from the Borg milling about drew their attention, and they turned in time to see Data approaching them.

Picard saw Riker and Worf both tense, but intuitively they waited to see what would happen and to let their captain decide what he was here to decide.

There was no punitive action, though, as Data simply walked up to them.

"Lore is no longer functioning," he said. Then he hesitated and obviously struggled to speak the rest. "He must be disassembled so that he will never be a threat again."

A passive face, glowing with the flush of effort—perhaps physically, perhaps not.

"It's good to have you back," Picard said.

Data looked at him squarely and simply said, "Thank you, sir."

Sensing the wisdom of leaving details unpursued for now, Picard turned back to Hugh.

"What will you do now?"

"I don't know," Hugh said. "We can't go back to the Borg collective . . . but I don't know if we can all coexist. We no longer have a leader here."

Picard regarded Hugh thoughtfully. "I'm not sure that's true."

It took Hugh a moment to realize Picard's meaning. "Perhaps in time, we can learn to function as individuals . . . and to work together as a group."

Thoughtfully, Picard nodded and offered him silent approval with his expression. His words had obviously not fallen on the ears of a robot.

"Good luck, Hugh," he said.

Hugh drew a long breath. "Good-bye."

Chapter Twenty-one

The Captain's Ready Room

"COME."

The captain's voice didn't sound very inviting, and under other circumstances, Beverly Crusher might have considered meeting with him at another time, but today she wasn't standing at his door as ship's surgeon. She was standing here as captain pro tem, and it was incumbent upon her to officially hand command back.

She'd waited for this. Oh, yes. To hand him back his starship, his crew of a thousand, his troubles, choices, and charges, and to run, not walk, back to sickbay.

Maybe she could do it through the door.

"Come!"

She leaned forward into the door's sensory sweep, and it rolled open before her.

There he was.

Friendly as ever.

Strange—she had always found him charming but never really needed him to be friendly. Not the way she needed it right now.

"Reporting as requested, sir."

"As ordered, Doctor," Captain Picard said roughly.

"Yes," Beverly sighed. "I understand." She presented herself squarely before his desk and made sure not to even hint at a desire to sit down. "Sir, please, let me speak first."

Picard's almond-shaped eyes took on a sudden sharpness at the corners as he looked up in surprise. He leaned back and folded his hands in a can't-wait-to-hear-this posture. "Very well."

"When you gave me command," she said, and had to stop to swallow, "I thought I understood what that meant. I believe all of us have an idea of command, but that idea never really fills out until we get a taste of it. We think we can do each other's jobs at the drop of a hat. We're trained to think that, but it's not true. Even though we did find a way to destroy the Borg ship, I disobeyed orders."

She paused to see how she was doing. Pretty well—his expression had mellowed, and his shoulders were down an inch.

"Yes," he murmured. "That's true. If you were a line officer, you'd probably receive a reprimand *and* a commendation for the same actions." He settled deeper into his chair.

She watched his face. The expressions were familiar, troubled.

"Beverly," he began, "I was quite . . . disenchanted when I learned that you had come back here. However, I must take the brunt of the blame. I chose to put you in command. Perhaps inwardly I was seeking your gentler instincts in a brutal situation. You did a very good job, but you were very lucky also. I'd prefer you hadn't risked my ship, however."

"Perhaps I shouldn't have," she said. "But, sir . . . you weren't there."

A smile pulled at his lips at the suddenly firm tone in her voice. "Yes . . . I wasn't there. I should have been. Command is a learning experience for both of us, Doctor. Perhaps next time—"

A woman who had been forced into the lion's den and had come to taste the love-hate addiction of command abruptly put out a staying hand. "No," she said. "No next time. I wouldn't want to come to . . . enjoy it too much."

The captain's smile flickered. All in an instant he understood.

Then the smile came back. "Besides," he said. "I would make a pitiful physician."

Belowdecks

Geordi La Forge, steeped with appreciation, walked down the ship's corridors.

Lucky guy. Blind from the womb, yet born in an age where blindness could be reduced to an annoyance—even used to expand a man's sensory capacity. Someday maybe a lot more people would be wearing these VISORS. After all the kinks got worked out . . . like some tyrannical nut being able to just walk up and take it.

Lucky to have friends and not just colleagues. Lucky to have survived.

Yeah, he was counting his blessings today. Eventually even the headache would be gone.

Just one more loose end to tie up.

"Lucky to be here to tie it up," he muttered, and tapped the chimes to a doorway.

"Enter."

The door parted and he strode into Data's quarters.

The cat meowed, and he turned in that direction.

Data was looking up at him.

"Hi, Data," Geordi said. He gazed at the android's face and saw the pulsing colors that showed him where every hot circuit was.

He moved closer.

Data was sitting at his desk, petting his cat and staring at a microchip on a glass slide.

"I just wanted to let you know," Geordi began,

"that Dr. Crusher says I'll be able to return to duty soon."

Data seemed to accept the little offering. Things could be made normal again. "I am glad that the injuries I inflicted on you are not permanent."

Geordi wanted to say something about that, about how those injuries were inflicted by somebody else. By Lore, by an aberration, by a bad dream—by somebody else.

Instead, he gestured to the slide.

"What's that?"

"This is the chip my father created for me so that I could experience emotions. I had it removed from Lore's body before he was dismantled."

The words were pretty plain, but something in them made Geordi nervous. Why did Data want this thing? All they needed was Data playing with poison again.

I don't want you altered by that thing, the engineer thought. *I just want you the way you are.*

But he couldn't bring himself to say any of it.

All he managed was "Does it still work?"

"No," Data told him passively. "I am pleased to say that it was damaged when I was forced to fire on Lore."

"Pleased?" George moved closer. Now he was really confused. "Data, you've wanted emotions all your life."

"Yes. But they were responsible for what I did to you." Data looked at him. He got up and crossed to a table. "I would never risk letting something like that

277

happen again. My friendship with you is too important to me."

With feigned matter-of-factness, he put the chip in a box and snapped it closed.

Geordi suddenly felt guilty. "I wouldn't be much of a friend if I let you give up on a life-long dream. . . ."

Data looked up at him curiously.

"Who knows, maybe one day we can repair this," Geordi told him with a smile, and he placed the box on Data's shelf.

THE STAR TREK

PHENOMENON

- [ ] ABODE OF LIFE
  70596-2/$4.99
- [ ] BATTLESTATIONS!
  74025-3/$4.99
- [ ] BLACK FIRE
  70548-2/$4.50
- [ ] BLOODTHIRST
  70876-7/$5.50
- [ ] CORONA
  74353-8/$4.95
- [ ] CHAIN OF ATTACK
  66658-4/$5.50
- [ ] THE COVENANT OF
  THE CROWN
  70078-2/$4.50
- [ ] CRISIS ON CENTAURUS
  70799-X/$4.99
- [ ] CRY OF THE ONLIES
  74078-4/$4.95
- [ ] DEATH COUNT
  79322-5/$4.99
- [ ] DEEP DOMAIN
  70549-0/$4.99
- [ ] DEMONS
  70877-5/$4.50
- [ ] THE DISINHERITED
  77958-3/$4.99
- [ ] DOCTOR'S ORDERS
  66189-2/$5.50
- [ ] DOUBLE, DOUBLE
  66130-2/$4.99
- [ ] DREADNOUGHT
  72567-X/$5.50
- [ ] DREAMS OF THE RAVEN
  74356-2/$4.95
- [ ] DWELLERS IN
  THE CRUCIBLE
  74147-0/$4.95
- [ ] ENEMY UNSEEN
  68403-5/$4.99
- [ ] ENTERPRISE
  73032-0/$5.50
- [ ] ENTROPY EFFECT
  72416-9/$5.50
- [ ] FACES OF FIRE
  74992-7/$4.99
- [ ] FINAL FRONTIER
  69655-6/$5.50
- [ ] THE FINAL NEXUS
  74148-9/$4.95

- [ ] THE FINAL REFLECTION
  74354-6/$4.99
- [ ] A FLAG FULL OF STARS
  73918-2/$4.95
- [ ] GHOST-WALKER
  64398-3/$4.95
- [ ] HOME IS THE HUNTER
  66662-3/$4.99
- [ ] HOW MUCH FOR JUST
  THE PLANET?
  72214-X/$4.50
- [ ] ICE TRAP
  78068-9/$4.50
- [ ] IDIC EPIDEMIC
  70768-X/$4.99
- [ ] ISHMAEL
  74355-4/$4.99
- [ ] KILLING TIME
  70597-0/$4.99
- [ ] KLINGON GAMBIT
  70767-1/$4.50
- [ ] THE KOBAYASHI MARU
  65817-4/$5.50
- [ ] LEGACY
  74468-2/$4.95
- [ ] LOST YEARS
  70795-7/$5.50
- [ ] MEMORY PRIME
  74359-7/$5.50
- [ ] MINDSHADOW
  70420-6/$5.50
- [ ] MUTINY ON THE
  ENTERPRISE
  70800-7/$5.50
- [ ] MY ENEMY, MY ALLY
  70421-4/$4.99
- [ ] THE PANDORA PRINCIPLE
  65815-8/$4.99
- [ ] PAWNS AND SYMBOLS
  66497-2/$5.50
- [ ] PROBE
  79065-X/$5.99
- [ ] PROMETHEUS DESIGN
  72366-9/$5.50
- [ ] RENEGADE
  65814-X/$4.95
- [ ] REUNION
  78755-1/$5.50
- [ ] RIFT
  74796-7/$4.99

822A-02

THE STAR TREK
PHENOMENON

- [ ] ROMULAN WAY — 74357-0/$4.99
- [ ] RULES OF ENGAGEMENT — 66129-9/$4.99
- [ ] SANCTUARY — 76994-4/$4.99
- [ ] SHADOW LORD — 73746-5/$4.95
- [ ] SPOCK'S WORLD — 66773-4/$5.50
- [ ] STRANGERS FROM THE SKY — 73481-4/$5.99
- [ ] THE TEARS OF THE SINGERS — 69654-8/$5.50
- [ ] THE THREE MINUTE UNIVERSE — 74358-9/$4.95
- [ ] TIME FOR YESTERDAY — 70094-4/$5.50
- [ ] TIMETRAP — 64870-5/$4.95
- [ ] THE TRELLISANE CONFRONTATION — 70095-2/$4.50
- [ ] TRIANGLE — 74351-1/$5.50
- [ ] UHURA'S SONG — 65227-3/$5.50
- [ ] VULCAN ACADEMY MURDERS — 72367-7/$4.50
- [ ] VULCAN'S GLORY — 74291-7/$4.95
- [ ] WEB OF THE ROMULANS — 70093-6/$5.50
- [ ] WOUNDED SKY — 74352-X/$4.50
- [ ] YESTERDAY'S SON — 72449-5/$4.50
- [ ] STARSHIP TRAP — 79324-1/$5.50
- [ ] SHELL GAME — 79572-4/$5.50
- [ ] WINDOWS ON THE LOST WORLD — 79512-0/$5.50

• • • • • • • • • • • • • • • • •

- [ ] STAR TREK: THE MOTION PICTURE — 72300-6/$4.50
- [ ] STAR TREK II: THE WRATH OF KHAN — 74149-7/$4.95
- [ ] STAR TREK III: THE SEARCH FOR SPOCK — 73133-5/$4.50
- [ ] STAR TREK IV: THE VOYAGE HOME — 70283-1/$4.95
- [ ] STAR TREK V: THE FINAL FRONTIER — 68008-0/$5.50
- [ ] STAR TREK VI: THE UNDISCOVERED COUNTRY — 75883-7/$4.99
- [ ] STAR TREK CONPENDIUM REVISED — 68440-X/$10.95
- [ ] MR. SCOTT'S GUIDE TO THE ENTERPRISE — 70498-2/$13.00
- [ ] THE STAR TREK INTERVIEW BOOK — 61794-X/$7.95
- [ ] THE WORLDS OF THE FEDERATION — 70813-9/$14.00

POCKET BOOKS